"These stories bring layer after layer of awe, humor, style, and vividness. Thompson-Spires's work stays with you."
—RAVI HOWARD, author of *Driving the King* and *Like Trees, Walking*

"An unusually intricate matrix of clear-eyed observation and devastating revelation about what it means to be a human being alive on this aching, raucous, unjust planet in the early twenty-first century. It is also, often, extremely funny, and is very smart on every page and gorgeously, rewardingly varied in its sentences and forms."
—LAIRD HUNT, author of *Neverhome*

"Dignified, controlled, and, above all, original: Thompson-Spires is an important new voice in contemporary fiction." —JAMIE QUATRO, author of *I Want to Show You More*

"With devastating insight and remarkable style, Thompson-Spires explores what it means to come to terms with one's body, one's family, one's future. The eleven vignettes in *Heads of the Colored People* elevate the unusual and expose the unseen, forming an original—and urgent—portrait of American life." —ALLEGRA HYDE, author of *Of This New World*

"The stories here are dazzling, wise, wicked, and tender. Nafissa Thompson-Spires's debut is a knockout."
—KELLY LINK, author of *Get in Trouble: Stories*

HEADS OF THE COLORED PEOPLE

HEADS OF THE
COLORED PEOPLE

Stories

NAFISSA THOMPSON-SPIRES

37INK

—

ATRIA

New York   London   Toronto   Sydney   New Delhi

37 INK

ATRIA

An Imprint of Simon & Schuster, Inc.
1230 Avenue of the Americas
New York, NY 10020

First 37 INK/Atria Books hardcover edition April 2018

37 INK / ATRIA BOOKS and colophon are trademarks of Simon & Schuster, Inc.

For information about special discounts for bulk purchases, please contact Simon & Schuster Special Sales at 1-866-506-1949 or business@simonandschuster.com.

The Simon & Schuster Speakers Bureau can bring authors to your live event. For more information or to book an event, contact the Simon & Schuster Speakers Bureau at 1-866-248-3049 or visit our website at www.simonspeakers.com.

Interior design by Silverglass Design

Manufactured in the United States of America

10 9 8 7 6 5 4 3 2 1

Library of Congress Cataloging-in-Publication Data has been applied for.

ISBN 978-1-5011-6799-7
ISBN 978-1-5011-6801-7 (ebook)

FOR IVEREN AND ISAIAH

CONTENTS

HEADS OF THE COLORED PEOPLE

HEADS OF THE COLORED PEOPLE: FOUR FANCY SKETCHES, TWO CHALK OUTLINES, AND NO APOLOGY

1.

Riley wore blue contact lenses and bleached his hair—which he worked with gel and a blow-dryer and a flatiron some mornings into Sonic the Hedgehog spikes so stiff you could prick your finger on them, and sometimes into a wispy side-swooped bob with long bangs—and he was black. But this wasn't any kind of self-hatred thing. He'd read *The Bluest Eye* and *Invisible Man* in school and even picked up *Disgruntled* at a book fair, and yes, they were good and there was some resonance in those books for him, but this story isn't about race or "the shame of being alive" or any of those things. He was not self-hating; he was even listening to Drake—though you could make it Fetty Wap if his appreciation for trap music changes something for you, because all that's relevant here is that he wasn't against the music of "his people" or anything like that—as he walked down Figueroa with his earbuds pushed in just far enough so as not feel itchy.

Riley was wearing the wispy swooped version of his bangs and listening to Drake or Fetty, and he was black with blue contacts and bleached-blond hair. And, yes, there are black people who have both of those things naturally, without the use of artificial accouterments, so we can move past the whole phenotypically this or biologically that discussion to the meat of things. And if there is something meta in this narrator's consciousness and self-consciousness or this overindulgent aside, it isn't meta for the sake of being meta; this narrator's consciousness is just letting you know about said consciousness up front, like a raised black fist, to get the close reading out the way and make space for Riley, who was the kind of black man for whom blue eyes and blond hair were not natural. He was the kind of black that warranted—or invited without solicitation—comparisons to drinks from Starbucks or lyrics from "Lady Marmalade" or chocolate bars, with nuts.

You would think with his blue contacts and unnaturally blond hair set against dark chocolate mocha-choca-latte-yaya skin—and yes, there is some judgment in the use of "you"—that Riley would date white or Asian women exclusively, or perhaps that he liked men. But you'd be wrong on all counts, as Riley was straight, and he dated widely among black women, and he was neither in denial, nor on the down-low, nor, like John Mayer, equal opportunity and United Colors of Benetton in life but as separate as the fingers of the hand in sex, nor like Frederick Douglass or many others working on black rights in public and going home to a white wife (and there is no judgment against Douglass here, just facts for the sake of descriptive clarity). Riley liked black women, both their blackness and womanness and the overlap between those constructs; nor was Riley queerphobic or the type of man to utter "no homo" in uncomfortable situations, because Riley was comfortable enough, if "enough" expresses a sort of educated awareness. There is so much awareness in these two paragraphs that I have hardly made space for Riley, who in addition to black women liked cosplay—dressing up as characters from his favorite books and movies—and *Dr. Who* and *Rurouni Kenshin* and the Comic-Love convention, and especially *Death Note*, his favorite manga and anime series. And though that day he was dressed as Tamaki Suoh (per his girlfriend's request), in a skinny periwinkle suit with a skinny black tie, his appearance gave him the flexibility to on other occasions dress as Kise Ryouta or Naruto, or, if he was feeling especially bold, Super Saiyan.

So it was bothersome, then, to Riley/Tamaki as he walked toward the Los Angeles Convention Center, when Brother Man at the corner of Figueroa and Fifteenth—not to be confused with the Original Bruh Man, whose actual origins or current whereabouts are unknown, but Bruh Man's gradated type, this particular yet stock Bruh Man, Brother Man—accosted Riley after he brushed away the pamphlet Brother Man was trying to hand him and put his hand on Riley's shoulder and ventured to violate Riley's personal space even further by using that large hand with cigarette-stained fingernails to turn Riley toward him. I am saying Brother Man stopped Riley on the street, singled him out in front of people dressed, respectively, as Princess Mononoke, Storm, Daleks, Cybermen, and Neil deGrasse Tyson (both in blackface and in their own black faces), put his hands on him, and forced him to look into Brother Man's own face with the familiarity of a friend yet, contextually, with the violence of a stranger.

On any other day Riley might have acknowledged that he was wrong to walk past Brother Man's initial "Howyoudoin," which he pretended not to hear on account of the Fetty. On this day, however, Riley felt that since he was inhabiting the character of Tamaki, his decision to ignore Brother Man was just right, an exercise in method acting.

Riley was more than surprised—and did not need to borrow Tamaki's affectations to feel slighted—that Brother Man had touched him, and by that point, even though he might have been just the kind of buyer for what Brother Man was selling, his pride wouldn't let him concede.

. . .

It had long irked Riley that his blackness or the degree of his loyalty to the cause should be suspect because he wore blue contacts and bleached his hair blond and because, on top of all that, his name was also Riley, and not, say, Tyreke. It irked him that he might be mistaken for a self-hating Uncle Tom because he enjoyed cosplay and anime and comic book conventions and because he happened to be feeling the character of a rich Japanese schoolboy a little too much at that very moment.

By the time Brother Man said, "Uppity, gay-looking nigga," Riley had bypassed logic and forgotten that he held none of the privileges of his costume.

There ensued then what Riley, in his costume, might have called fisticuffs, though in everyday life he would have simply said they got to scrappin, right on Figueroa Street.

The people who watched and filmed and circulated the scene from inside one of the lobbies of the convention center said it was just like Naruto v. Pain, only with two black guys, so you couldn't tell if either one was the hero.

2.

In truth Brother Man was burly but not violent and rather liked to regard himself as an intellectual in a misleading package. If he could have made a wish before the end of that day, it would have been that he, too, had worn a costume to soften the effects of his image.

When he put his hand on Riley's shoulder, it was only because he disliked the sight of someone, especially one of his own, turning his back to him without hearing him out. It was also because he needed to promote *Brother's Spawn* and had thus far convinced a meager four passersby to buy a $4 copy that day, and because Brother Man felt, unapologetically, that black people should stick together and that the blue-eyed, wig-wearing brother in the purple suit should have at least acknowledged him with a nod, if not a handshake or a howyoudoin.

Though in the aftermath, people would call his papers religious tracts, indoctrination materials, and "some kind of gang documents," *Brother's Spawn* was Brother Man's self-published dystopian comic series set at Pasadena City College, where he first learned of Octavia Butler and her work. The comics were hand-drawn with the dimensions of a postcard, though he also hoped to sell broadsides featuring a poem he had written.

Brother Man—aliases Kyle Barker, Cole Brown, Overton Wakefield Jones, Tommy Strawn, and pen name Brother Hotep—was selling the postcard comics illegally (he preferred the term "without official city permits") between a food truck and a juice cart that day. On other days he sold them near the Century City Mall, in Ladera Heights, in Little Ethiopia, and as far as Inglewood.

That day, he banked on the convention center's Comic-Love traffic and the potential readers it might attract, boasting to his girlfriend earlier in the morning that he would probably sell out, "even without one of those official tables in the convention center, watch."

And though he would say he was not usually the type to call Riley a sellout or an Uncle Tom, that day, Brother Man (real name Richard Simmons, yes, Richard Simmons) could not handle Riley's refusal to acknowledge him or his art. He could find reasons to dismiss the hundred or so people in costumes, some speaking English, some other languages, who shook their hands no at the laminated mock-ups he tried to show them, but he could not abide a black refusal, especially one from a black guy in a Japanese prep-schoolboy costume, the very kind of audience Brother Man hoped to cultivate.

Thus, when he put his hand on Riley's shoulder, he never meant to hit him, and if he could, Brother Man, hereafter Richard, would have imagined that Riley didn't plan to fight him either. And neither man ever would have thought that amateur karate (pronounced in the authentic Japanese accent) would be involved, their arms flailing and legs kicking out in poorly choreographed mortal combat.

3.

On his way to a meeting, Kevan stopped at the SweetArt Bakeshop in Saint Louis to purchase a vegan brownie for himself and a purple cupcake with tiny candy hearts for his daughter Penny, who was with him for the weekend. The whole shop was lined with canvases of varying sizes, painted by the owners and sold from the bakery, which served as a gallery and community meeting space. Tiny vases holding local flowers adorned each table. Kevan wore a black T-shirt that said in white letters, "Eff Your Respectability Politics." He liked the irony of the word "eff" instead of the F-word, but he still debated whether it was better to change "your" to "yo." He wasn't sure if anyone understood the stakes in these decisions or in any of his other art, which he sold online, from his car, and occasionally from a small suitcase in the barbershop on Washington Avenue.

He had one hour left with Penny before her mother would pick her up so Kevan could meet a potential business partner and pitch an idea that he couldn't shake.

He chose a table in the middle of the nearly empty shop, with yellow-and-green flowers in the vase. "She's a superhero," Penny said, pointing to the largest canvas on the wall adjacent to the bakery case, and inhaling another glob of frosting. The frosting accumulated at the corners of Penny's smile, but her tongue missed those spots each time it swept her mouth.

"She's cute. Daddy can teach you to paint like this," Kevan said, passing Penny a napkin across the table.

Kevan wasn't a vegan, but he supported black business and black art, and regarded SweetArt as a place where his own work might one day be represented. The T-shirt sales provided him a stash of petty cash, but Kevan had sold only three paintings, and that grieved him. He supported his daughter Penny with a court order and a "real job" as a UPS deliveryman, but he "always took care of my responsibilities," even before Penny's mother, whom he alternately called a gold digger, that whore, and my queen, demanded official monthly payments.

"My superhero name is gonna be"—Penny paused to pull back the wrapper and expose the last quarter of the cupcake, its frosting smooshed and all the candy hearts gone—"my name's gonna be Purple. Purple Penny Powers. I will make things purple like this," Penny said, zapping something with her arm.

"Purple Penny Powers." Kevan pretended this was cuter than it was. "Wow."

He was trying not to think about a joke he had seen earlier in the day, trying not to remember the sight of two dead bodies that had appeared casually in his news feed, trying to rehearse instead his pitch for the realization of something he had read in a book that he found in a used bookstore.

The Afric-American Picture Gallery was a series of written sketches by William Wilson, under the pen name Ethiop and following the form of similar sketches—which Kevan found with more research—by James McCune Smith in *The Heads of the Colored People* and Jane Rustic (a.k.a. Frances Ellen Watkins Harper, a black abolitionist poet and suffragist). Kevan wanted to commission painters, including mostly himself, to create a full exhibit of heads of the colored people, now and then, to take the written, literary work and render it visually. The idea intrigued him, the heads talking to him like the books in Equiano—though he didn't know that reference yet.

In Kevan's collection, there would be, as in Ethiop's original, Phyllis Wheatley, Nat Turner, and a doctor, but he would update his favorite sketch, "Picture 26," of the "colored youth" who was "surrounded by abject wretchedness" to reflect a sort of current abjection. To these he would add a superhero for Penny and a collage of the black men (and women, he would concede, with some coaxing later from Paris Larkin) who had been killed by police and other brutalities.

"Now what's your name going to be?" Penny's voice seemed especially shrill at the moment.

"I don't know." Kevan was still thinking about the bodies and the grainy video of the two men arguing and the way one of the men had held out his hand when the police officer entered the scene; it was clear that the man wasn't holding a gun or a knife, but something soft, like paper.

"Daddy, your name," Penny demanded.

"I don't know," Kevan repeated, and blurted out the first thing that came to his mind: "Bruh Man."

"Bruh Man?" Penny jutted her head back. "What does he do?"

"He paints, and whatever he wishes, he can paint it and make it happen." Kevan made Penny lick a napkin so he could wipe the leftover icing from her face. "And he can make bad things un-happen, if he paints them right."

"That's gonna be my power, too," Penny said, pulling away from his grooming and hesitating in the way of five-year-olds, "but I'm just gonna think and make it happen or unhappen."

He wished briefly that things were so simple and then began to outline something on a napkin.

4.

Paris Larkin was meeting Riley at the convention center after two shifts at her part-time job for Dark Shadows Hollywood Cem-etery Tours. Her official job description said, "Tour Narrator: Vocal talent. Must be able to memorize stories and stand for long periods of time on moving bus while engaging audiences." I ain't saying she a gravedigger, Riley liked to begin when he introduced her as his girlfriend, but really, she digs graves, like, loves them. It was one of the things that had attracted him to her when they first met, her dark cheeriness and her nonjudgmental approach to his lifestyle. And his soft-landing punch lines were one of the things Paris liked about him, and his interesting face, and the way he wasn't at all who she expected him to be.

When he took his contact lenses out at night and tied his hair down with a durag, Riley looked just as comfortable and kind as when he dressed up and hung out at his favorite comic café in Pasadena, drinking boba tea and playing chess with kids from Caltech, where he studied engineering and was one of a handful of black students on campus.

If Paris could have a superpower, it would be to make herself visible, because even though she stood at the front of the bus with a microphone, pointing out alleged sightings of Marilyn Monroe to hungry tourists with camera phones and fake Gucci sunglasses, she wasn't the main attraction, and she preferred to narrate the tours with reverence instead of theatrics, to fade into the background and let the spirits speak for themselves. With Riley she could be seen, since they got a decent amount of attention when they were together and especially when they dressed up. Certain cosplay purists (read: racists) did not always approve of Paris's or Riley's respective costume choices or the idea of black people dressed as nonblack characters. Paris had come to anticipate and almost enjoy the surge of anxiety that came with entering these spaces, had felt her flight-or-fight instinct the closest thing to being fully alive. And the ghost tours, too, made her think that by comparison, she was at least more alive than the bodies that filled those holes.

That day was not her day off, so she took the Metro and two buses to meet Riley at the convention after work, after showering and changing into her long silver wig and meticulously sewn necromancer dress, her dark skin contrasting with the purple-and-white pinstripes of the dress, the gray armor on her arms and legs elevating her mood. She had debated dressing as Haruhi Fujioka, the counterpart to Riley's costume from *Ouran High School Host Club*, but her choice of Eucliwood Hellscythe created a bigger impact, she thought. Though she kept her blue contacts down and focused on her sketchbook, her eyelids, adorned with heavy black-and-white shadow, warned other transit passengers to dare her, that day.

When Paris entertained visitors from out of town, or when she and Riley caught the spirit, she liked to ride the Metrolink from Highland Park to Glendale to visit Michael Jackson's mausoleum, which you couldn't exactly get close to, but which still sent a melancholy shiver through her and her guests. During most of her time on the bus or the Metrolink, Paris drew Riley and many other people—you could call her a sketch artist, though not in any official, paying capacity.

She called her sketchbooks a collection of heads, for she never drew bodies, and anyway, Paris was lighthearted and laughed frequently, showing the gap between her teeth, not nearly as morbid as her job and curated heads make her sound. She called Riley Fuzzy Lumpkins, and he called her Bubbles. She was listening to "Say My Name," attached as she was to all things nineties, even though she was nineteen and had been born after Tupac and Biggie were already dead. That morning, Paris had watched reruns of *Martin* and laughed at a character's plea for a wish sandwich. In the nineties, she felt—and you should fill in for yourself a kind of longing here—something melancholy, plaid, flannel, but not overwrought.

It isn't true, at least not in Paris's case, that you can sense what the future holds. That day, she had jokingly, in an exercise of character acting, avoided pronouncing Riley's name near the word "death" or at the graveyard or while dressed as Eucliwood, lest she kill him. But no psychic, metaphysical force warned her to tell Riley not to go to Comic-Love or to avoid arguments without spoils or to immediately put his hands up when instructed to do so. Nothing told her, still humming "Say My Name" in her best humming voice, not to walk toward the large crowd of flashing lights, police cars, and costumed and uncostumed bystanders. Her stomach urged her to look away, once she got close enough to be sickened, but she couldn't then.

She didn't feel more alive from the surge of panic in her body or in comparison to Riley on the ground.

Years later, she would regret not drawing the offending officer that day. Since then, she has sketched his face over and over, penciling his name and image in her notebook as a sort of plea, saying it aloud, wishing that she, like Eucliwood, could pronounce the names of those she wanted to die and make it so.

When an artist named Kevan Peterson wrote to her about a project he wanted to finish—really, to finally begin—Paris was glad for her sketches of Riley.

5.

A well-read, self-aware, self-loving black man with blue contact lenses and blond hair and a periwinkle suit was shot down in Los Angeles after a reportedly violent altercation with a well-read street promoter, who was also shot, after police officers answered a complaint. "Who was also shot" here signals the afterthought that was Brother Man, Richard, because he was not the one with the blond hair or blue contacts or in any way exceptional, except for his size and the things he had overcome (too many to name here), and his comic books.

And you should fill in for yourself the details of that shooting as long as the constants (unarmed men, excessive force, another dead body, another dead body) are included in those details. Hum a few bars of "Say My Name," but in third person plural if that does something for you.

A few more points I should not leave to the imagination: in the chalk drawing on Fifteenth, you can see Riley's leg kicking out like Spike Spiegel and an additional rectangle above the outline of Richard's hand, where he might have held his comic books or a laminated mock-up.

The picture the Associated Press chose came from a Throwback Thursday photo that Riley had posted on social media, a picture of him in a costume from an undergrad party, at which he wore an oversize blue shirt and a bedazzled blue bandana over cornrows. His mother, and girlfriend, Paris, explained repeatedly that he was not dressed as a thug, but as nineties Justin Timberlake.

Brother Man's picture was an old mug shot, accompanied by a story that emphasized a criminal charge from five years ago—for child support nonpayment and tax evasion—and his penchant for false names.

Both men's families would say the pictures didn't say anything, that that's not how anyone who knew them would remember them.

The Neil deGrasse Tysons disagreed over the number of gunshots they heard; the one in blackface said ten, while the one with a brown face called black said thirteen. The autopsies would not conclude, but there might have been marijuana in Riley's or Richard's systems, at some point.

6.

I think a cop shooting is too melodramatic when the story was interesting on its own, and my preoccupation with race is perhaps overdone, but it was O'Connor, I think, who said—and I say "I think" here more as a device, to affect a sort of nonchalance, when in fact I know she said—everything that rises must converge or something like that ("or something like that" serving as another affected clause). But that makes the ending sound intentional or overdetermined, when it wasn't, though I believe—I know—it was Donika Kelly who said "the way a body makes a road," or in this case an outline, impression.

. . .

How to end such a story, especially one that is this angry, like a big black fist? The voice is off-putting. All the important action happens offscreen; we don't even see the shooting or the actual bodies or the video. Like that one guy in fiction workshop said, meta is so eighties. The *mise en abyme* is cool but overdone. This is a story of fragments, sketches. Dear author: Thank you for sharing this, but we regret.

I concede that it might have been so much more readable as a gentle network narrative, with the cupcakes and the superheroes and the blue eyes and the nineties image-patterning. But I couldn't draw the bodies while the heads talked over me, and the mosaic formed in blood, and what is a sketch but a chalk outline done in pencil or words? And what is a black network narrative but the story of one degree of separation, of sketching the same pain over and over, wading through so much flesh trying to draw new conclusions, knowing that wishing would not make them so?

THE NECESSARY CHANGES
HAVE BEEN MADE

Though he had theretofore resisted the diminutive form of his name, in his new office, Randolph felt, for the first time, like a Randy.

If Randolph were truthful, he could admit that he began acting like a Randy months before Isabela and especially the week before the holiday. That Tuesday, after Isabela had wished him a tepid "Happy *Than*sgiving" and he was sure she was gone for the weekend, Randolph had picked up the little silver picture frame on her desk and spit-washed her face and meager breasts through the glass, swirling his index finger until she blurred into a mucoid uni-boob. He returned the frame, packed his things into two blue copy-paper boxes, and shuttled them to his new office, hoping his bonsai would survive the transition and the dark holiday. Even with the lamps he purchased, the room was dim, but he was determined to keep the fluorescents off. His new office sat at the back of a musty corner near the janitorial closet, but it was, he reassured himself, *his* musty corner. He drove home for the break pleased with his victory and the progress and restraint he showed in achieving it.

Before Isabela, DIY had been the subject of Randolph's irritation, and before DIY, Crystal, before Crystal, Fatima, and before Fatima, Randolph's mother, the Virgin Mary, and a girl who sneered at him in second grade.

. . .

Before Isabela, when Randolph was first hired at Wilma Rudolph, an HBCU, the department chair, Carol, had introduced him to Dr. Ivan-Yorke, saying that he should meet with her at least twice during the semester so that she could provide a letter for his file. Other than the fact that Randolph and DIY were two of the only three black professors in the department, he wasn't sure why he was assigned to Ivan-Yorke. She didn't work in his specialization and hadn't written anything of note in decades. Her eyes sat high on her head and deep in her face, which, because of its plumpness, reminded Randolph of gingerbread dough. Randolph had seen her the day of his interview limping down the narrow hallway in what he described later to his friend Reggie as some sort of funereal muumuu but which at the time struck him as a plain black dress.

"This is Dr. Randolph Green, a new assistant professor," Carol had said, "from Preston." Dr. Ivan-Yorke glared coolly down her square glasses before lifting her head slightly and gesturing for Randolph to examine the collection of office mugs displayed on her shelves. Randolph's glance—for he was astute at times—picked up a DIY theme. One mug, lavender with white lettering, said, "Keep Calm and Do It Yourself." Another said, "A Job Is Never Done until *I've* Done It." Carol looked at him apologetically, laughing a little. "That's right. I forgot to tell you that everyone here calls Dr. Ivan-Yorke 'DIY.' Her favorite saying is—"

"Do it yourself," DIY interrupted, with one flaccid arm raised toward her collection.

"Ha," Randolph forced.

"Come closer," DIY whispered. "I've been here for over twenty years."

There was no one in the hallway or the nearby offices. Randolph didn't understand why she spoke so quietly.

"I've read some of your work," DIY mouthed. "Why did you leave the prestigious Preston?"

"You know," Randolph said. "Wanted to try something different." He didn't say what he told others: that he wanted a reprieve from performing his status as an antistereotype or that he needed a break from the beneficence of liberal guilt, all eyes on him, the expectations of smiling, gesturing women. He felt one of his migraines already. They started in the small indentation at the base of his head, where neck meets pituitary cavity. The veins constricted as though a nylon cable were forcing the blood up, up, and out of his forehead. Pressure flooded the ocular nerves, concentrating itself behind one eye or the flat bone around his temple. He saw no aura, only felt the violence of it all.

"You know how it is," Randolph repeated.

"I don't," DIY said, turning back to her desk.

Carol and Randolph saw themselves out of the office.

. . .

Randolph hadn't wanted to share an office any more than he'd wanted to teach at a historically black university, but Wilma Rudolph was the only other university in the city and was the only one still looking for an advanced assistant professor in the late spring, and by then he'd have done anything to get away from Preston and what he and Reggie called its "tyranny of whiteness." It turned out, to Randolph's dismay, that while the students at Wil U were mostly black, the faculty was nearly as homogeneous as Preston's, especially in the humanities. The school, he felt, was run almost entirely by women, and Randolph came to understand them as an unholy sisterhood of pseudofeminists, with DIY as their unofficial leader, Carol their henchwoman-in-training, and Isabela their likely successor. A black man, he told Reggie, was just as much a token there as on the other side of the city.

The consolation prize for the job was his double office with the most enviable windows in the building. The other nontenured faculty members were housed in two slums on the third and fourth floors of the building, sitting five or six people to spaces that should have been called carrels. But the two faculty members who'd shared the office previously had left on short notice, bequeathing to Randolph a large, well-lit space of his own. Until Isabela.

She was hired in late September, a month into the school year, after the department chair of Spanish and Portuguese received complaints from students that their class was unassigned to an instructor. A professor from the Spanish department walked into Randolph's office with a woman at her side, gestured toward the partition and second desk, and told Isabela, "This will be yours," before she introduced herself and Randolph's new office mate. Isabela smiled in a way that most people, including Randolph, would perceive as warm, and asked his department.

"English, literature really." Randolph smiled back.

"Oh, good. You will help me. I'm from Venezuela. My writing in English is not so good."

"Well, neither is my Spanish," he'd said with a laugh.

"This is my first time teaching in the States," she said. "I taught in Venezuela."

"It's my first time teaching at an HBCU, too." Randolph wanted to make that clear.

"It's a beautiful campus, very green," she said.

"It's a campus," he said.

She smiled and nodded for a reason Randolph couldn't interpret, then began to unpack the little rolling suitcase she had brought. Randolph showed her where to find office supplies, how to adjust the thermostat, which had a tendency to stick, and how to sign up for the university's text-alert system. At Preston, crimes on or near campus were summarized in a monthly email from PR, probably to minimize the sense of widespread criminality, though the numbers were likely similar to Wil U's. At Wil U, crimes were part of the daily tableau. Alert: reported sexual assault on the fourth floor of Wiley. Alert: students robbed outside McGill. Alert: black Mitsubishi Gallant stolen from West Featherringhill parking lot. Sometimes students sounded like they were going to fight in the hallway. Once, two faculty members did. The anxiety didn't even register for Randolph anymore, he said, but he thought Isabela, especially as a woman, should be prepared.

Isabela, however, seemed almost unfazed as Randolph told her the stories. She nodded, her eyes serious as he spoke. "The school where I taught in Caracas is very violent."

"Hmm," he said. "Where I grew up was rough, but I didn't expect it at a university, even one in the South or in the hood." He put the word in scare quotes. "Ghetto?" he asked, unsure if she understood.

She shrugged and twisted her lips, as if to say she'd expected it. "People are the same, where you put them."

Randolph shrugged this time. He finished the tour of the office by telling Isabela that he liked to keep the lights off because of a sensitivity to artificial light and, he emphasized, because of the great windows in the room. The office faced south and was fully lit until the late afternoon most days, the trees outside providing just enough shade so that the sun never felt sharp. She nodded slowly, her lips pursed. He continued, "We can close the office door if things get too loud in the hall."

Randolph realized as soon as the words left his mouth their potential for misinterpretation. He should probably keep the office door open, for her sake, for the sake of propriety. He watched her face for discomfort and found none. Still, he started to explain that he hadn't meant anything, but she just said, "Yes, I don't like lots of noise."

He thought they would be friends. They were about the same age, unmarried and content with that status. Randolph didn't want to date another coworker, and Isabela, he said, wasn't his type anyway, though Randolph's friends would say that wasn't true. He wouldn't even meet with his former coworkers at the Preston campus, for fear of running into his ex Crystal, a history professor who said that Randolph's passivity belied chauvinism and that his book proposal, *The New New Paternalism: Romantic Racism and Sexism in the Post-Postracial Era*, would continue to go nowhere until he confronted his own masculinity issues. Crystal confused Randolph, because she wanted him to be angrier, scarier in bed, bought him books on erotic asphyxiation, called him Smaller Thomas during an argument, and concluded that he had low T, but broke up with him after he got "too rough." She couldn't have it both ways, he argued. "You always overcorrect or undercorrect, but never get it just right," she cried.

When describing Isabela, then, Randolph oversold her undesirable aspects: She was not unattractive, but flat, bland yet aggressive. She wore her brown hair in a ponytail, which accentuated her ears. All her features were tiny—her ears like those of a little old man, and her nose, a narrow point with a slightly beaked end—yet overpronounced.

Isabela, he later learned, wanted to settle into life in the United States, maybe find a tenure-track job, before dating. It was a perfect situation for maintaining a platonic relationship, which Randy insisted he wanted. They both felt underdressed among the students, who alternated between church and club wear to classes. They laughed easily. She ate trail mix from a Ziploc bag. Randolph ate granola mixed with M&Ms. They kept their respective desks tidy and arranged their bric-a-brac just so. They shared disbelief at their students' general boldness.

. . .

One rainy day in mid-October, Isabela sighed, a bit dramatically, Randolph thought. She must have had an altercation with a student, but when he asked, she said, "Randy, it is very dark in here today. May I turn on the lights?"

Randolph considered how to answer. He didn't want this to become a pattern. "Oh," he said. "Well, remember, I keep them off because I can't deal with the fluorescent bulbs. I get migraines." He pointed to his chestnut-colored forehead and frowned.

She nodded. "Yes, but it is very dark."

"It's fine today, I guess. I'm leaving soon, but in general, I prefer not to have them on." Randolph fiddled with his necktie.

She turned on the lights. The department chair, Carol, stepped into the office as Randolph packed up his bag.

"Oh, Randolph, I'm glad I caught you," she said, her face flushed, though it always looked that way. "I was going to email you, but I was walking by the office anyway. Dr. Ivan-Yorke says you two haven't officially met for a mentoring session. Remember you need to meet twice each semester. I wouldn't wait too long. You know how it is after the break."

"I'll get on that." Randolph fake smiled.

"Great. Hi, Isabela," Carol said before she left. "How're you liking the office?"

"It is very nice with the lights on," she said, looking at Randolph.

Carol paused, and glancing at Randolph said, "I suppose it would be."

Randolph didn't know what to make of Isabela's comment at the time, so he focused on Carol's. He'd avoided his mentoring meetings because DIY struck him as another nut among many in the school's canister. Though he was six feet three, he felt something shrink in her presence.

· · ·

A few days after the first time she requested more light, on a day that Randolph did not recall as particularly overcast, Isabela beat him into the office, and when he arrived all the lights were on. He sat down at his desk and considered how he should approach the situation. Perhaps she didn't understand the severity of his medical problems. He could call her over to his desk and pull up a Wikipedia page about migraines. He could say, in Spanish, that he really preferred natural light to all this fake stuff, which changes the rhythm of the brain and disrupts work. He could tell her that he'd been generous by using headphones, instead of speakers, to listen to music, so the least she could do was let him leave the lights off.

He said, pantomiming an expansive space, "The windows are very big, bright, don't you think?"

She said, "Yes, but an office without lights? It is very strange. It doesn't look nice."

"What about a desk lamp?"

"Desk lamp." She spit the words out like they were made of metal.

"It's a little light that sits on your side of the office, for overcast days."

"I know what it is. I will think about it," she said, turning back to her computer. She did not offer to turn off the lights. "It is cold in here," she said, pulling her sweater around her chest.

· · ·

When Reggie called Randolph that afternoon to check on him, Randolph tried to describe the environment accurately, starting with DIY. "She's at least seventy and limps along the hallways with a cane, flashing warnings at visible and invisible offenses. She's not the department chair, but you'd think so," he said.

"Sounds like Black Crazy personified," Reggie said, though he said that about nearly anyone he saw as overworked, and about most female academics who happened to be black. Reggie had served as Randolph's assigned faculty mentor at Preston through the Minority Mentoring Program. He was about ten years older than Randolph, and had written a book called *Black Crazy: Tipping Points in Black Literature, 1874–1974*. He took Randolph to lunch once a month, observed his classes a few times, and wrote a recommendation letter that would sit in his Interfolio queue should Randolph choose "not to fool around after this little experiment is over and get a real job at a research university."

"She's Black Crazy all right. I'll tell you about her later. But look, Reg, I want to pick your brain about my new office mate."

He described Isabela as "a wall with a nose," hoping to avoid a lecture.

"Good. I've told you before—"

Reggie repeated his stock advice, the same advice Randolph's parents and all his other mentors, formal and informal, repeated: "Don't screw it up. Err on the side of passivity. Don't date anyone in the humanities departments. Don't even look at those women's legs when they pull out their short skirts in the spring or when they prance up the stairs in those leggings." Lost in his lecture, Reggie failed to give Randolph any useful suggestions about the light situation.

Randolph assured him that there was no chance of him dating Isabela and said goodbye. Before he hung up, he heard an incredulous "Mhhhm," though Randolph supposed he could see why Reggie wouldn't believe him. At Preston, Randolph had broken two of Reggie's rules at once by dating Crystal—both colleague and white woman—and a third when he told him he wanted to take a break from the research setting and get a teaching job at a liberal arts school for a couple of years. "You're on your way to Black Crazy," Reggie said with a shrug. "If your students don't kill you, the four-four load will."

The teaching load was heavier than Randolph expected, even after hearing Reggie's stories of lost colleagues and "scholars who showed so much promise early on," but the environment bothered Randolph the most, the cramped classrooms, the oldness of the place, its sharp luminance. In meetings, Randolph pouted while DIY sat on her elevated chair whispering, the women leaning in, straining to hear her. That's how they all were, Randolph concluded, making you lean into them and accommodate their every whim, their eccentricities. Randolph had begun to hate the whole lot of them.

· · ·

When he returned to his office—their office—after class the next day, the door was open and the lights were on. Randolph thwacked his folder and a stack of papers on his desk without looking at Isabela.

"You can turn the lights off," she said without looking up. She was wearing one of those sweaters with a low-cut oval neck that usually look good on really skinny girls, yet somehow it did not, Randolph insisted, look good on Isabela.

"Oh, no," he said. "It's fine."

"No, I did not know if you were gone for the day or for a class. It's okay." She frowned, nodding toward the light switch.

"I'm only going to be here for a few more minutes. It's fine." Randolph fumbled through his desk drawer for a bottle of Aleve and his prescription pills, looking from one bottle to the other, as if making a decision about which level of migraine he had. He rattled the pills around and poured one into his hand. He could feel her mouth mocking him, even with her head turned, her little beak scrunching up.

"It's a real condition, you know," Randolph started, loudly, "overillumination. I literally get headaches from these lights, all fluorescent lights."

"Hmm."

He pointed to his head. "You've never had a migraine, I guess."

"No. It's okay, turn off the light."

· · ·

Randolph asked his three o'clock class how they would deal with "an inconsiderate roommate who, for instance, made a lot of noise while you were trying to sleep."

Someone said, "Mind games."

Another said, "Man, I'd tell him to keep it down. When I gotta study, I don't have time to play."

"Just ask for another roommate," someone else said.

"Like that would work," several people seemed to say at once.

. . .

On Monday, he got up twenty minutes early to beat Isabela into the office. When she came in, she smiled and said hello as though nothing had changed between them. Randolph made small talk, taking the opportunity to build a bridge, if a bridge is defined as the path to getting one's own way.

"Would you like me to get you the desk lamp?" he started. "You know, this was my idea, and I feel bad about adding an expense. I can buy the lamp." That sounded fine, he thought, not too pushy, but hopefully rhetorically manipulative enough to remind her of the gravity of the situation.

"That is fine." Her mouth went from neutral to something else. They didn't speak again that day.

. . .

The morning Randolph presented her with the lamp, in what he hoped was a cute mosaic pattern, Isabela did not smile. She paused with tight lips and said, "Thank you," leaving the lamp untouched.

She beat him to the office for the next couple of weeks and turned on all the lights except her desk lamp. Whenever one left, the other adjusted the lighting to his or her preference. Randolph researched overillumination, looking for ways to convince Isabela of her insensitivity. Two of the friends he polled said he was making a big deal out of nothing; she probably just didn't understand. Two other friends said she was being a jerk, and there was no way she could misunderstand. Jerry, a mutual friend of Reggie's, said, "This is the kind of petty drama that can only happen with a woman. She's the aggressor, but watch out now, or she'll make it all look like your fault." Reggie said this was about power and that Randolph could only lose, whichever way he played it. If he acted aggressively, he became what "they" always knew he would be, and she won. If he let her have the office, she won. "How do you think I went from Reginald to Reggie?" he said. "You can't win, brother." The Richter needles in Randolph's temples charted small hills.

What else could Randolph do? He'd tried reasoning and compromise. He fantasized about driving Isabela out of the office, delighting in her expression at the sight of a fake rat spinning in her chair or a Spanish-English dictionary on her desk. He'd seen people on reality television rub their testicles on their housemates' mattresses or pillowcases and brush the inner rim of a toilet with their toothbrushes. The victims never found out until they met for the reunion episodes and watched the footage together. Randolph wasn't ready to pull his balls out over this, nor did he like the way they could implicate him in a potential misreading of the situation, but he thought about it.

. . .

One late morning while she was still in class, Randolph went over to Isabela's desk and flattened the bag of trail mix she always kept there, crunching a few of the nuts with his thumb and watching their oil streak the plastic. As quickly as he could, he removed all but a few of the yogurt-covered raisins and put them into his pants pocket. He flicked the desk lamp on and off three times and returned to his desk to eat the raisins before they melted into a mess, the cream and hydrogenated oils thick and sweet against his gums.

When he returned from class, Isabela was out of the office, and a book called *Microaggressions* had been left on Randolph's desk. He tossed the book to her side of the office, not caring where it landed. When he pulled his lunch bag out of his desk drawer, he found his sandwich spotted with four abnormally large dimples on each side of the bread, like deep fingerprints. Randolph removed the bread from his sandwich, placed it back into the paper bag, and ate the smoked turkey directly from the plastic.

At his urban middle school in Chicago, a kid was shot for allegedly stealing someone's lunch. At Wil U, a faculty member was caught going through another one's desk drawers, and a fistfight broke out in the hallway. The woman won. At Wil U, a boy had been jumped for leaving the library at the wrong time. At Preston, Randolph found that people with money committed these assaults but left fewer traces, the violence psychological. He heard stories of girls saturating tampons with ketchup and sticking them into other girls' thousand-dollar handbags. They published anonymous glossy newsletters accusing male professors of roving eyes or worse and tucked them into faculty mailboxes. Caracas or not, Isabela didn't know how Randolph's dual schooling had prepared him to get ugly. She didn't know with whom she was fooling.

In fact, Randolph would call his problem one of duality, twoness, though not in the purely DuBoisian sense, but in the sense that he was of two minds about most things, and very few of those things converged. He maintained two social media pages, one for colleagues and one for old friends who knew him when.

Both included the phrase "it's complicated" under his name. Reggie would say that the tyranny of whiteness both emasculated him and expected him to adopt hypermasculinity. Randolph could find no nonbinary position on the continuum. He could only flip-flop.

. . .

Randolph didn't tell Reggie about his sandwich or the raisins, but he told him that the migraines were getting worse, even with the dose of amitriptyline he'd been prescribed. Reggie said, "Those headaches will go away once you stop feeling like you have to be some kind of standard, once you just let it all out. The problem is once you do that, you won't have a job. For me it's nosebleeds. I call 'em my monthly cycle. The pressure has to come out some kind of way."

. . .

On a Tuesday, while Isabela and the lights were out, Randolph sneaked over, again, to her side of the office. She had apparently hidden the trail mix, because it was not in sight. In the silver-framed picture on her desk, she hugged her toddler nephew and wore a red cocktail dress. Randolph fingered the floral-print cup that held her collection of number 2 pencils, most of them yellow and sheathed in those soft cushions that slide over the top. He pulled the sheath off one of the pencils and squished it around in his hand. The pencils were freshly sharpened, the goldenrod, brown, and black contrasting attractively. Randolph took a sheet of Isabela's scratch paper, then used each pencil in succession, dulling the lead by pressing hard as he drew little spirals, each stroke of the pencil a little ecstasy. He hid the blackened paper in his messenger bag and removed any dust or traces of broken points that had landed on the desk and rearranged the pencils as he remembered them. He didn't want to be the next blip on the text-alert system. Alert: robbery and assault in office of non-tenure-track female faculty member. Suspect: tall black male, generally thought handsome, accused of keeping the lights off in a suggestive manner, eating fourteen yogurt-covered raisins, and breaking a desk lamp and eleven pencils.

He returned to his own desk, locking up the blackened scratch paper, his lunch, and all his office supplies. He noted the spot where the blue edge of his bonsai's pot lined up with the silver crack in the file cabinet.

. . .

The Monday before Thanksgiving, Randolph arranged a mentoring meeting with DIY, hoping to feel her out about the potential for a new office. He planned to discuss his upcoming annual review and then to casually bring up the situation with Isabela. He knocked and stepped into the office carefully, but she whispered, "Just have a seat. You don't need all that false formality with me. How is your semester going?"

"It's okay, an adjustment."

She watched Randolph's face too carefully, for too long, before she said, "You don't like that office mate, do you?"

Randolph laughed, debating whether he should tell her the truth, unsure what she would do with it. "I just don't want to make her uncomfortable," he started, and felt compelled to apologize for this dishonesty, "but actually she's making me uncomfortable." DIY didn't stir. He looked away from her eyes; their cloudiness reminded him of marbles you might trade away.

"You're a woman," he began again, feeling like a liar, for her femaleness seemed, to him, buried far beneath the nest of thinning hair, the severe black clothes. "I don't want it to look bad, you know, like I'm doing some kind of exercise in male domination." He chuckled.

DIY made a *pfff* noise with her mouth and leaned back before she leaned in. She took deep inhalations from the back of her throat and exhaled the words without parting her teeth. "That's your problem," she said. "You're afraid of the light."

He started to speak, but she gave him a withering look.

"You think you're too good for this school. It's obvious to me. You don't want to be exposed, so you overcorrect in some places, but it all comes out somewhere else."

"I don't think I follow," Randolph said, the word "overcorrect" pinching his ego.

"That's one of your other problems." She paused her rebuke for a moment before trying again, "There's this saying in law, 'mutatis mutandis,' 'the necessary changes have been made.' It doesn't apply to you."

"And how exactly is this relevant?" The veiled hints and analogies were too much for Randolph's migraine.

"Sometimes the problem is the environment; sometimes you *are* the environment. In your case, you think you're making changes, but you take the problem with you, like you did exchanging your old job for this one." She gestured with one hand for him to leave.

Randolph left the meeting furious with DIY, though he couldn't put his finger on exactly why. He asked Carol about the new office that day, and though it looked like another demotion of sorts, it represented, for him, a battle he won, growing a pair.

· · ·

As he walked out of a faculty meeting one wintery afternoon, Randy paused near the adjunct who'd moved in with Isabela, a skinny guy with adult acne. "How do you like the new office?"

"It's good," he said. "Nice windows."

"Why do you guys have the lights off? Are you a migraine sufferer?"

"No, Isabela's idea," the adjunct said. "She gets really hot, so she keeps them off. You know, boiler's right under us."

BELLES LETTRES

Dr. Lucinda Johnston, PsyD
Johnston Family Therapy
1005 Knightcrest Rd, Claremont, CA 91711

TUESDAY, OCTOBER 1, 1991

Hello Monica,

I'm sure you remember me from the class field trip to the Getty in
September. It has been brought to my attention by Mrs. Watson
that Fatima may have started a nasty rumor about my Christinia.
I hope to clear this up, as we both know how ugly these things
can get. It is true that Christinia's hamster died recently, but it is
absolutely not true that it died at Chrissy's hand. At no time has
Chrissy ever put Hambone or any of her previous hamsters in the
microwave, dryer, or dishwasher. What kind of child would make
up something like that?

It sounds—and I say this respectfully, so I hope you won't be
offended—like Fatima has had a very hard time getting acclimated
here, and that's understandable, but I do hope you will deal with

her before any such incidents become frequent. Children who start
lying young often end up with longtime patterns of dishonesty.

All best,
Dr. Lucinda Johnston, PsyD
Licensed Therapist
Welcome Wagon, Westwood Primary School
Events Coordinator, Jack and Jill, Claremont Branch

• • •

Monica Willis, PhD
Associate Professor of Education
University of La Verne
1950 Third Street, La Verne, CA 91750

MONDAY, OCTOBER 7, 1991

Dear Lucinda,
I apologize for my late reply, but I only found your letter at the
bottom of Fatima's backpack when I did my weekly cleaning.

Thank you for writing to me, though I have already spoken with
Mrs. Watson, who made it very clear that she never heard Fatima
say a thing about Christinia or her dead hamster(s). It was Renee
Potts who claimed that Fatima started the rumor. Fatima says she
only repeated what Christinia herself told her.

Many of Fatima's stories about Christinia this year and last—
which I won't recount here—have been disturbing to say the least,
but none as disturbing as Christinia's enjoyment of torturing rodents.
Fatima has a strong imagination and writes beautiful lyric poetry—
which she started reading at age four—but she does not have a

history of lying or telling gruesome stories. And unlike Christinia, she has no history of running off with other girls' shoes while their feet dangle from the monkey bars. I'm absolutely sure that Fatima wouldn't tell stories about Christinia, the hamsters, or the microwave incident if they weren't based on something Christinia had said first.

I appreciate your concerns about Fatima, and even though Christinia has made it much more difficult for her to find friends at Westwood, Fatima will acclimate soon. She's going to a sleepover at Emily's this weekend. Is Christinia going? If so, I hope you will encourage her to play nice.

Best,
Monica Willis, PhD

P.S.
It is true that liars who start young often end up with psychological and social problems of the sort that Christinia has demonstrated over the past year. How lucky for you (and for Christinia) that she has access to psychotherapy through your practice.

. . .

Dr. Lucinda Johnston, PsyD
Johnston Family Therapy
1005 Knightcrest Rd, Claremont CA 91711

MONDAY, OCTOBER 7, 1991

Dear Monica,
I never expected so much defensiveness when I wrote my original letter. Perhaps you misread it. All I wanted to emphasize is that

I understand why a girl in Fatima's position and one with her background would make up such stories. It's hard to get attention in a new place, and Christinia has been established at Westwood for quite a while. There is probably some petty jealousy going on, but I think we can resolve this. I don't know how you did things at Fatima's old school (in Fresno, was it?), but here we try to help the children work through their problems without getting too involved.

I suppose you already know—and have known all along—that Christinia will not attend Emily's party, so there's no need for me to encourage her to "play nice." You've probably heard that history already, so I won't rehash it, but I will say that it wasn't Chrissy's fault that Emily broke her nose when she fell. Besides, it was three years ago. We've given the Kemps our sincerest apologies for Emily's unfortunate accident, and we have moved on.

Finally, and I say this respectfully, but maybe it would be wise to go through Fatima's backpack every night instead of once in a blue moon. I have heard from more than one parent that it smells like eggs.

My best,
Dr. Lucinda Johnston
Licensed Therapist
Author of *Train up a Child*
Welcome Wagon, Westwood Primary School
Events Coordinator, Jack and Jill, Claremont Chapter

. . .

Monica Willis, PhD
Associate Professor of Education
University of La Verne
1950 Third Street, La Verne, CA 91750

OCTOBER 9, 1991

Dear Lucinda, or should I say Dr. Johnston,
I'd like to resolve this as much as you would, but that won't happen
if all of your letters begin and end with backbiting. I asked about
Emily's party sincerely and in good conscience, though after speaking
to the Kemps, I can see why they would hesitate to invite Christinia.
I would ask you to consider this, however: If Fatima is the problem,
why is she growing in popularity while Christinia is only growing in
girth and the number of casualties associated with her name?

I'm not of the mind that the only two black children in the class
should be enemies, nor do I like the attention it draws to them (or their
parents) when they're already in a difficult position. I would think
that a black woman of your stature and success would understand
how isolating work and school environments like Westwood can be
for people like us. Jordan and I hesitated to send Fatima to a PWI, but
we know the benefits of a school like Westwood. I hoped Christinia
and Fatima could be friends and could support each other in this
space, but it's been clear since second grade that you and Christinia
are not willing to make that work. You could encourage your child to
be cordial, however, and less brutal. You could spend more time with
her so she doesn't lash out at others. You should get the help you both
need in overcoming your tendencies toward pettiness.

I'm sure Fatima would let Christinia into her growing inner

circle—even her after-school reading club—if Christinia would only apologize and behave. Jealousy can become a lifelong problem. On that note, I hate to bring this up now, but we were surprised by how poorly Christinia behaved when Fatima's poem won over hers last year. I'd like to make sure we don't end up with a repeat performance of that tantrum when the poetry competition rolls around this year.

As for the hard-boiled egg, we resolved that last spring and bought Fatima a new backpack. And I believe you knew that already.

We should talk about some concrete ways we can encourage our girls to get along. Perhaps Mrs. Watson can help, since she has mentioned Christinia's problematic behavior before, something to the effect of, "If we don't fix things now, she'll have a hard road ahead of her."

Cheers,
Dr. Monica Willis, PhD
Author of *Every Voice Counts: Helping Children of Color Succeed at Predominantly White Schools*

. . .

OCTOBER 9, 1991

Monica,
Excuse the informal note.

Mrs. Watson told me herself at Pavilions that "it doesn't matter how brilliant the child is. No one will ask about her grades later in life, but they will want to know how well socialized she was." She made it no secret that she was referring to Fatima, not Chrissy.

And to that point, I think you're doing both yourself and

Fatima a great injustice by continually emphasizing her "brilliance" over other children. Lots of people skip grades, and skipping kindergarten isn't something to brag about. I doubt that the standards at her old school were as rigorous as those at Westwood. What exactly was she advanced at, naptime? Maybe a stint in kindergarten would have cultivated her social and problem-solving skills so she wouldn't run home and tell her mother everything. Children need strength of character and independence, after all.

If you'll recall, moreover, I was there at the recital where Fatima read her "award-winning poem," and while my doctorates—yes, plural—may not be in literature, I'm pretty sure hardly anyone would call "Butterfly Pie" a work of poetic genius. You can't rhyme "pie" with "pie" multiple times and call that poetry; you just can't, even if you have the excuse of only being in fourth grade.

We are not self-conscious about Christinia's blackness. I attended Westwood myself as a child and was very happy there, even though at the time I was the only black child in the entire K–6 division. Perhaps the kids at Fatima's old school were bad influences on her? Why did she change schools after first grade anyway? That's generally a bad sign.

Isn't your degree, by the way, an EdD?

—Lucinda

. . .

OCTOBER 11, 1991

Lucinda,
It's hard to believe you're not a brain surgeon with your manifold doctorates and strong sense of logic. Fatima changed schools

because we moved. Was she supposed to commute from Claremont to Fresno every morning so she could attend her old school?

I'm not surprised if Fatima's subtle wordplay was lost on you, since it's clear reading problems run in the family. Fatima said she saw Christinia struggling in the Panda reading group, and Mrs. Watson hinted that the Iguanas—Fatima's and Emily's group—are reading much more advanced work than *Charlotte's Web* or *The Boxcar Children*. Fatima started on *Little Women* during her own free time and has read through a number of Judy Blume and Beverly Cleary works, even *Ellen Tebbits* and *Otis Spofford* (which I read as a much older girl). And, Fatima has a poem coming out in *Ladybug* magazine in a few months.

Not everyone is suited for literary work. I'm sure you know that from your own writing struggles and the extra effort you had to put behind your research in order for anyone to take it seriously. Isn't there still some kind of issue with your last project and the IRB, or is the issue with Dr. Patel's ex-wife? I know someone who might be able to clear things up for you, if you'd like the help.

My very best,
Monica

• • •

OCTOBER 11, 1991

Monica,

Mrs. Watson said there is absolutely no reading group higher than the Panda group, and that the Iguanas have been paired to minimize their various social anxieties, so I have no idea where you're getting the notion that Fatima's reading is more advanced than Christinia's.

Chrissy has no social anxieties, and if she's ever struggled socially, it's because other children don't understand her. And Chrissy read that abridged version of *Little Women* just yesterday on the way home from soccer practice. The pictures took up more space than the words.

But now I see where Fatima's delusions of grandeur come from. You are, unfortunately, enabling your child's arrogance and stifling her growth even at this young age. I write about this very thing in chapter three of my first book, *Caution with Coddling*.

There is no trouble with my current research or the Institutional Review Board.

Regards,
Lucinda

• • •

OCTOBER 11, 1991

Lucinda,
Christinia may not have notable social anxieties, but that is because she dominates the other children. There has to be some insecurity behind that, perhaps about her size. I heard (and I won't reveal the source, lest you start harassing her, too, but I can tell you it was not Fatima) that Christinia steals other kids' lunch scraps from the cafeteria and bullied that poor kid with the unfortunate ears into giving her all of his pepperoni for the next month.

I really hope that in addition to help for her lies and early signs of psychosis, you will get Christinia some help for her weight problem before she ends up—and I say this respectfully, so I hope you won't be offended in the least—like you. Children do pick these things up from their mothers.

If by your "first book," you mean your unpublished dissertation, I've heard plenty about it and the unsavory circumstances of your defense. Wasn't Dr. Patel married when he joined your committee and divorced by the end of it? Is that why you say your oldest child, Thaniel, has "good hair" and why Christinia is always bragging about having "Indian in my blood," despite those naps in her head? I thought she meant a different kind of Indian, but now things are clearer. Does Mr. Johnston know those may not be his children, or is he in on the ruse with Dr. Patel?

Take care,
Monica

•　•　•

OCTOBER 12, 1991

Monica,

I'm not going to dignify most of your comments with a response.

This will be my last letter, because I can see I'm not going to get anywhere with you; there's some kind of blockage there that I really think you should explore with a licensed professional, especially if you call yourself a professor. How many generations of college students will go on to harm others because of your bad pedagogy?

It's funny to me that you would try to reactivate those rumors about my strictly professional working relationship with Dr. Patel, especially since we've all heard things about Fatima's biological father. Let's see: three kids, two of them with Anglo names, and one with an Arabic one; two kids with Mr. Willis's features, one kid (Fatima) with a more "African look." Mathematically speaking, it seems you picked up more on your travels to Africa than those seventies-style caftans you insist on wearing.

To your point about Chrissy's weight, we are working with a children's nutritionist who specializes in lymphatic disorders.

At one time I wondered if we were too harsh in recommending that you and your family wait another year before joining our Jack and Jill chapter, but I can see now that we were right. I'm afraid I can never recommend you for our club. You display a volatile combination of residual ghetto and uppity Negress, and that will be your undoing, if Fatima isn't.

Sincerely,
Dr. Lucinda M. Johnston
Licensed Therapist
Author of *Train up a Child*
Welcome Wagon, Westwood Primary School
Events Coordinator, Jack and Jill, Claremont Chapter

. . .

OCTOBER 13, 1991

Lucinda,
I'm not even going to respond to that.

But I will say that if someone here is uppity, it's the one of us with two little brats who have run off three au pairs. Who even uses that term? If they're not French (and I'm pretty sure your cousin Shaquanna isn't) they're nannies! Nannies! And if they're your own relatives, then they're just babysitters or bums who need a hookup.

This bourgieness and the way it keeps you from connecting with your kids is half of your problem; the other half, you probably can't fix without medication. Good thing you can write prescriptions. Oh wait, you're not that kind of doctor.

I've been forthright about Fatima's biological father, but I certainly don't appreciate Christinia's relentless and uneducated use of the phrase "African booty-scratcher."

And how can I be "uppity" when I've never had any help and started out as a single parent before marrying Jordan? If putting myself through school and becoming the highest-educated person in my family with no help but God's makes me uppity, then so be it. We are humble people, in spite of our education and finances, and we have more class in our excrement than you have in your whole hamster-murdering family.

And yes, there is a bit of the ghetto still left in me, enough to tell you who can finish the fight if it gets to that point. We're never too far from Oakland or the Southside.

Let's keep it real,
Monica

. . .

OCTOBER 13, 1991

Monica,
I do believe that was a threat. The Claremont Police Department will not take this lightly.

While I don't approve of Chrissy's use of the term "African booty-scratcher," she was only stooping to Fatima's level when she used it. As they say, if the butt itches . . .

I don't know where you get this "African folklore" Fatima has been spreading around the school, but I should think that no educated person would tell stories of the Mamie Waters who will "snatch you baldheaded" if you go underwater. It took me hours to console Christinia and convince her that her delayed hair growth is unrelated to her swimming lessons or any mythical African mermaids.

And tell Fatima to stop pinning notes to the inside of Chrissy's bookbag when she's not looking. Chrissy could injure herself on a dirty safety pin, knowing you people, and end up with hepatitis A, B, or C, or worse. And tell her to stop harassing Chrissy with pitiful insults about her appearance and "dark-skinded self."

I've tried to resolve our differences by working directly and exclusively with you and Mrs. Watson, but I will have no choice but to contact Principal Lee—in addition to the police—if this persists.

—Lucinda

• • •

OCTOBER 14, 1991

Lucinda,

Only you would suggest something so disgusting as intentionally injuring a child with a dirty safety pin, but then again, it was Christinia who put that tack on Renee Potts's chair last year and caused her to need a tetanus shot. Perverse minds think alike, apparently.

I can say with complete assurance that Fatima would never make fun of someone for being too dark, nor would she use the word "skinded" in a sentence. In fact, she came home crying last year when Christinia called her blacky, but I told her to forgive Christinia.

Jordan and I have never raised Fatima or any of our children to be color struck, and that's part of why we would never participate in an organization such as Jack and Jill. We only applied because we thought we might find like-minded black friends here, but if you are their representative, we'll pass. The paper-bag test may be long gone, but the slave mentalities are not. And your Chrissy is baldheaded because you don't know how to do your own hair, let alone hers. Don't blame the Mami Wata for any of that.

Now I see that Christinia is blaming Fatima for many of the things she (Christinia) is doing herself. You probably haven't read that Shirley Jackson story "Charles," have you? I would imagine it's too difficult for you to process, but sometimes children—especially those who don't get enough support at home—do these things.

Lose my number and address, and stop making your kid do your dirty work,

M

. . .

OCTOBER 14, 1991

Monica,
Turn blue.
Turn blue.
Turn blue, blue, blue.

Look, I've written a poem. Perhaps I should send it to *Ladybug* magazine.

Love,
Lucinda

. . .

OCTOBER 15, 1991

Lucinda,

You need Jesus. Do not write to me again, or I will contact my lawyer.

I've asked Mrs. Watson to check Fatima's backpack for correspondence from you, and I have made it clear that I do not want further contact from you or Christinia. You are not to speak to Fatima either.

Monica

Jack and Jill
Claremont Chapter
1402 Wedgewood Ave, Claremont, CA 91711

. . .

Drs. Jordan and Monica Willis
730 N. Briarwood Ave
Claremont, CA 91711

OCTOBER 15, 1991

Dear Drs. Willis,

We would like to formally invite you and yours to our annual Jack and Jill Gala, October 25, 1991. Attire is black tie. Please respond using the enclosed notecard. We hope to see you there.

If you have received this invitation, it is in error.

Anonymous

. . .

OCTOBER 18, 1991

Lucinda,

I'm beginning to think you are insane. There is absolutely no way that Fatima called Christinia's grandmother (may she rest in peace) the "b" word, nor did she call her a "batch." And I'm sure she never said, "I'm glad she's dead." We don't expose Fatima to bad language. Our child is not the one who brags about killing hamsters and putting them on roller coasters to see if their eyes pop out.

It's a shame you and Christinia have so much trouble writing and reading, because these stories could rival the best of any true-crime stories out there. And that fact should scare you, because it's the ones who start out with rodents who eventually graduate to the babies and the grandparents, may they rest in peace (!). Where will Christinia be in ten years, and do you want to see her get to that point?

I'm requesting a meeting with Principal Lee, Mrs. Watson, and you and Mr. Johnston so that we can nip this crazy mess in the bud once and for all.

Monica

Drs. Jordan and Monica Willis
730 N. Briarwood Ave
Claremont, CA 91711

. . .

OCTOBER 21, 1991

CC: Michelle Watson

Dear Mrs. Johnston and Mrs. Willis:

It has come to my attention that your respective daughters, Christinia and Fatima, engaged in a brutal fistfight at school. As you know, this behavior violates not only the Westwood code of conduct, but also our core values as a school, and is punishable by expulsion.

I am sending this letter as a follow-up to the discussion I had with each of you over the phone. I would like to meet with the two of you and Mrs. Watson ASAP. My secretary will schedule.

Sincerely,
Principal Lee

Albert Lee, Principal
Westwood Primary and Secondary School
201 Highland Hills, Claremont, CA 91711

. . .

Drs. Jordan and Monica Willis
730 N. Briarwood Ave
Claremont, CA 91711

OCTOBER 25, 1991

Dear Drs. Willis:

The school's board and I thank you for your generous donation and for agreeing to serve on the Westwood Welcome Wagon. Given the sharp improvement of your child's behavior, we can agree to rescind our threat of Fatima's expulsion from school.

The reputation of our school depends on the efforts of involved parents like yourself.

Sincerely,
Principal Lee

. . .

NOVEMBER 3, 1991

Lucinda,
Thank you for inviting Fatima to Chrissy's party. She will be happy to attend.

And thank you for the lovely fruit basket. You are so bad! It's true—Mrs. Watson looks terrible in that color, and yet Principal Lee finds reasons to look. But I won't say anything more in writing.

Jordan and I will discuss the Jack and Jill potluck with you when we see you.

XO,
Monica

THE BODY'S DEFENSES
AGAINST ITSELF

The back of the woman's neck is already sweaty. Liquid pools in the dark creases behind her ears and around the collar of her oversize T-shirt. She is wearing loose sweatpants, the cotton kind, and thick white socks to class. She stands at the back of her mat, scratching one ankle with a big toe, turns around suddenly, and smiles. I avert my eyes, annoyed by her expectation of familiarity, and focus on aligning the front edges of my mat with one of the faint slats in the polished hardwood. I watch her face in the mirror. She could be a distant cousin, her nose not unlike mine, but she is fat.

The room always smells damp before class even starts, misty from the deep exhalations, drained lymph nodes, body odor, and steam that the previous students left behind. Bodies fold and unfold, adjusting themselves in quiet discourse in the heated space. The new woman struggles through Eagle Pose, even with one foot tucked around an ankle. Biniam steps behind her, places a hand gently on her back, and says, "You might do better if you remove your socks." I can't see her feet in any detail after she balls the socks and sets them down, but I imagine white cotton lint clings to the deep brown of her skin. I lift my foot higher and press my heel into the space where my thigh meets pubic bone. I am wearing short briefs and a sports bra, the typical uniform for the women in this class. If the new black woman is self-conscious about the bagginess of her clothes and body, her face, pleasant, does not let on.

"Relax your face," Biniam says to me. I try to unclench my jaw, letting the sweat run down my forehead and bare arms. The woman is watching me in the mirror. I close my eyes.

. . .

The summer I turned eleven, my body would not stop sweating. Before then, I welcomed the Inland Empire's dry heat, imagining myself a brown lizard, sunning myself on a flat rock in red sunlight, camouflaging, until my parents called me inside the house with lectures about heat stroke. It's the kind of heat I still miss in humid, foliaged Nashville. Nashville is more like the Bikram studio I attend there, damp all year round. Upland, California, isn't really damp, except in the morning when the fog hovers. It can be cold in the winter, but a dry, quiet cold. In the valleys, there's no elevation to carry the heat, so the cold settles over everything like more dust.

My sixth-grade classmates, noticing my sudden hyperhidrosis, and led by Christinia, called me Sweatima. Fatima Sweatima. I seemed to be the only one who sweated through the cold as much as the heat. I sweated through daisy-print dresses and sunflower T-shirts. I sweated through jackets and coats that I kept on all day to hide the sweat. I sweated through a sweaty cycle that only made me sweatier and more ashamed of the sweat and sweatier still as I tried to hide it.

"It's anxiety," a doctor said, but neither my mother nor I would have agreed to a pill to quell my nerves back then. "Is there a history of trauma?"

My mother and I looked at each other and back at him and shook our heads in unison. Maybe it just had to do with being in that specific body, a body so different from everyone else's at school, one that wouldn't do the things that other people's did or that did too much of them. I would try harder to relax, my parents and I concluded.

"'Be a thermostat, not a thermometer. Don't be reactive. Be a thermostat, not a thermometer. Thermostat. Thermostat. And hold on.'" Mom's voice merged with Wilson Phillips's, forming the soundtrack to our daily commute. The perspiration usually started each morning between Fairwood and Rio Road, as we turned the corner and traveled the block toward school. I had double anxiety, anticipating the trials of the day, and the unrelenting moisture that left all my shirts permanently marked with green-and-yellow stains. I would make a mental list of possible retorts, canned answers for the insults that would undoubtedly dart toward me at some point during the school day. The list never helped.

I wasn't good at coming up with retorts, even if I practiced them beforehand. I had my stock "whatever," which came with a head turn and an eye roll. And I had, "Hmm, maybe you're projecting," something I'd picked up from talk radio. And I had self-righteousness, loads of it: "One day you're going to be sorry that you didn't take the high road like I did." That never worked. The high road is too abstract; kids can't see it, and really neither could I. I could only hold on for one more day, grasping at the idea of retribution because there was little else

I could grasp. The best comebacks always came to me in my bedroom, hours later, when I sat watching reruns of *The New Mickey Mouse Club* or *Kids Incorporated* and brooding over the day. And wishing that when I lifted my arms, they were as dry as Stacy Ferguson's or Rhona Bennett's.

That year, I'd managed to get through the first months of school without any major incidents. But by the late fall in a seventh-period math class, I experienced the worst trial by far. Christinia had come around to sharpen her pencil, she'd claimed, but she'd bypassed the sharpener attached to the wall and stuck her nose near my coat with a look of self-satisfaction and disgust on her face. It was the kind of coat with fur around the hood and far too warm for me or for that day. My mom had insisted that I wear it because of the chill in the air, and once the sweat started, I kept it on despite the warm classroom.

I never understood how Christinia decided to choose her target each day. I wasn't the only one, but I was her favorite—the only other black girl, the one with the special name, the girl who sometimes insisted on wearing eighties clothes in the nineties. When I met her in second grade, I assumed that Christinia and I would be friends. We had skin color and intelligence in common, and our mothers were both doctors, and my mother wanted me to have a black friend, black friends plural if there had been more options. She said it would round out my experience, but really, I think it was one of the ways she could justify putting me in an otherwise white school. But Christinia and I were different. She was the kind of black girl who wore fake hair, something I could never do, and who bragged about having "Indian in my blood" to white listeners who seemed bored or amused but clearly unimpressed. Her stomach made her one of the heftier girls in the class, and when I got up the courage to look down on her, I made a point of flaunting my thinness—the only desirable thing about my body—over her tendency toward chubby. People could make up their nicknames, but I made sure no one would ever call me Fati, Fatty.

. . .

Biniam leads us through Garudasana (Eagle Pose) and Sputa, which sounds like a dirty word in Spanish, but which means Fixed-Firm Pose. Biniam is vaguely African—Eritrean, Ethiopian—with a thin nose and thick, shiny curls. He says, in that accent that women find attractive, "Fatima, relax the shoulders, soften the gaze." With the new black woman, there are three of us in this class. She flops down flat on her soft stomach instead of taking a vinyasa on the way to Down Dog, collapses instead of hovering. Once, Biniam said, "Fatima," dragging out the last syllable, "that name is honorable; you should look up its history." I know its history.

"Turn your gaze inward," he says, making his way toward me. I try, but I watch the woman. Her eye catches mine again. I look away.

. . .

I don't know if it was the differences between our bodies or the one similarity that made Christinia hate me on first sight. But she expressed her disdain for me in the five years that followed in sporadic, disjointed ways that were interspersed with kindness. The unpredictability amounted to emotional abuse. One day she'd pull up my shirt in front of the entire class and reveal the pink undershirt that should have been a bra, and the next day she'd give me a really expensive present, like the Hello Kitty pencil box from the Sanrio Store with all the compartments and the matching erasers.

"I wish I had some good tweezers to make this easier," she'd said once as she helped me remove the splinter from my clammy hand after an accident on the balance beam. I barely felt a prick when she pinched the skin around my palm and then held up the tiny wood between her index finger and thumb. "Got it."

"That wasn't bad," I said, examining the tiny pink hole Christinia had left in my palm.

She paused then and grabbed my hand again. "You have a lot of calluses," she said.

"Monkey bars. Remember in elementary? I used to play on them every day."

"My mom says calluses are the body's defenses against itself," Christinia said. Her mother wasn't that kind of doctor—she had a PhD, like my mother, and they both let everyone know it—but Christinia was a walking medical book. She paused, still holding my hand. "I can read your fortune," she said.

"I don't believe in that stuff." I backed up, taking my hand with me.

"Just real quick," she said.

Warmth passed between us and she ran her finger over my palm.

"You're going to die young," she said with seriousness in her face.

"Where does it say that?" I pulled my hand away again to search it myself.

She laughed. It was a throaty, almost phlegmy laugh with a shrill edge. *Hihihihi*, like she used the wrong vowel. Who laughs with an *i* sound instead of an *a* or an *e*? "You're so gullible!" she yelled and ran off.

Later that school year, we wrestled, in a fight that almost got us both expelled—for the second time—over her accusation that I thought I was better than she was. She made me feel confused and unstable. I avoided her; she sought me out.

The day she sniffed me, I heard her coming. As she approached the pencil sharpener, she made the kind of noises she always made when she set out to make fun of something. I heard her horse-whinny *hihihi*, the same sound she'd made in second grade when she, on her way to sharpen a pencil, convinced Rhianne to stick the tack on Renee Potts's seat. She made the same whinny the next day when she found out that Renee had to get a tetanus shot.

I know I didn't smell like Teen Spirit. No deodorant can completely eliminate the odor produced by a combination of excessive sweating, excessive anxiety, an excessive coat, and the hormones an eleven-year-old body produced. But I was still surprised when, like ants, my classmates one by one made their way to the pencil sharpener and sniffed me on the way back to their seats, carrying over their heads the words "musty," "gross," and "so weird." I sat frozen in a cold sweat, imagining myself somewhere else. Mrs. Trebble never directly let on that she noticed, but she gave me a piece of candy, a half-melted Hershey's Kiss, after class.

The whole thing was more embarrassing than the time I had to leave the classroom because I was upset by the Holocaust movie. It was even more embarrassing than when I misread Jason's kindness and asked him to be my boyfriend and when he kindly said no offense, but no. It was worse than all those things because it said something about my inherent inability to be something normal, to be a girl, to be perfect all or even some of the time.

My whole body burned that day, but I didn't cry in front of them. I never cried in front of them. I pretended not to hear the whispers and snickers, and Emily pretended with me. We ate lunch with our mouths quiet and our eyes tapping code. "Don't feel too bad," Emily blinked. "Everyone knows Christinia's a jerk."

"Easy for you to say, since she never bothers you," I blinked back.

With her mother's help, when Emily got home, she would wonder why her only friend was the sweaty black girl with the weird name. Tomorrow, we would pretend it had never happened. Christinia would utter the nickname Sweatima, which would spread like wildfire across the lockers and hallway, under the guise of saying hello. Then she'd move on to bothering Renee or someone else for a while.

· · ·

Biniam says to get into Pavanamuktasana, Wind-Removing Pose. He is attractive, maybe gay. Some of the white women in the class preen for his attention, showing off or pretending to need help. If he is interested in them, he never lets on. His facial expression, a vague smile, does not change. He treats the new woman perhaps a little more gingerly than the rest of us.

· · ·

The summer I turned fifteen my body would not stop bleeding. I had "accidents" at school even when I wasn't on my period, one of which culminated in a crimson stain on the back of my shorts and Christinia pointing and laughing as I walked—as naturally as I could—from our table in the cafeteria to the girls' bathroom with Emily's sweatshirt tied around my waist to hide the mess and Emily walking behind me to shield me from anyone else's view.

My mother asked gently, but with fear in her eyes, "Have you done anything with anyone? Anyone?"

In an algorithm that made sense only to my mother and grand-mother, any physical contact with a boy was inherently sexual, and any sexual contact was fecund. Thus hand-holding led to penetration, which led to pregnancy, which sometimes resulted in miscarriages—the only explanations they could imagine for my abnormal bleeding—in the same way that a dream about fish meant someone in the family was pregnant.

"No," I repeated three times before her face softened, and two times to the female OB-GYN who asked me the same question, once with my mother in the room and once after she asked my mom to step out for a moment.

I was terrified of having a pap smear after reading about them in *Seventeen*. I couldn't imagine what investigating a pregnancy entailed.

"I haven't even held hands with anyone," I said to the doctor. She had smooth brown skin and long black hair. My visible shame seemed to settle the matter for her; with my virginity established, she could treat me like a person instead of just a body.

When she called my mother back into the room, she said, "Fatima's a good girl. I think this is related to her diet. It doesn't seem like the vegetarian thing is sustainable the way she's doing it. She needs more green leafy vegetables." Then to me, she said, "Are you eating enough?"

In high school, on a good day, when she decided we were friends, Christinia sat across from me in the cafeteria. Emily flicked her brown hair and exchanged an eye roll with me, but despite the blood incident, I wasn't anxious around Christinia anymore, though I was still anxious more generally. I had lengthened out into somewhat tall and something like pretty, but I still couldn't get a date at my school. Christinia had grown from baby fat to a more mature obesity, but she seemed smaller in high school, in the bigger crowd. She sat with me and Emily and some of our friends sporadically; she had so few friends of her own that I almost felt sorry for her. I began to view her as a benign growth with the ability to flare up every now and then but with no real power.

I proceeded to eat my standard lunch of Funyuns and Diet Coke, making each little onion ring last for five bites. I wasn't exactly vegetarian for health reasons, and despite the gynecologist's advice, I don't think I ate a green vegetable until my twenties.

"They say people who become vegetarians young are just hiding eating disorders," Christinia said, taking a bite of something brown and wet that came on a Styrofoam plate.

"Who says that?" I asked, looking at Emily.

"Medical studies. My mom said." Christinia slopped a bite of the brown meat and sauce.

"You and your mom might try eating less meat, or just less," I said, and Emily and I dragged out our laughter, consciously, until it spread across the table to the other girls. I prepared for a confrontation with Christinia, a sequel to our previous fights, but it never came. I winced when I saw the quick flash of pain in her eyes and watched her walk away from the table.

• • •

The new woman shows surprising balance when it's time to transition from Warrior Three to the standing split. She does it with an effortless lift of her right leg.

• • •

The summer I turned nineteen, I no longer needed my fingers or a spoon to empty myself after eating. I could not retain big meals.

With the hyperhidrosis under control, my body found other ways to purge; it learned how to punish itself.

. . .

"Forearm stand," Biniam says, "but only if it is part of your practice." He looks toward the new woman. "You can practice Three-Legged Dog or move to a wall so I can spot you." Some of the women in the class begin to spread their arms in front of them, like cats leaning back for a stretch. I have managed forearm stand once at home, without the aid of the wall, and a few times in Biniam's class with the wall and his support. I don't know what has gotten into me today, why I am more competitive than usual. I prep for the pose, pushing my weight into my forearms, tighten my core, lift one leg a foot or two off the ground until it hovers high above, bring the other to join it in the air.

I find the pose, clenching my stomach muscles to support me. I delight in my ability to lift myself up this way. I can't see the new woman, but I feel she is watching from the safety of Child's Pose.

I don't know how long I have held myself in Forearm Stand; it could be five seconds; it could be a minute. Sweat pours from my forehead onto my mat in the space between my two perched arms. I look forward to Savasana, where we will lie very still and focus our awareness on "being in this body." My arms give out, and I try to regain my balance by "activating my core." One leg flops to the side. I try to land in Wheel Pose, but the fall is so sudden that my body and brain disagree about their directions.

. . .

Last summer, when I turned thirty-three, my body started bleeding again, and the stress from that has revived the sweating problem. Nothing traumatic precipitated this change, and the absence of that trauma is somehow traumatic in its own way. I have been eating fine, well even, so many green smoothies, so many salads, very few grains. I avoid all the glutens. My husband and I had decided I should try getting off the pill, which I convinced my mother to put me on after another accident in high school, so that we could prep for trying to conceive. The pill dried up the bleeding for sixteen years, but it dried up all my other juices as well. Now I'm supposed to be "detoxing," cleansing myself from synthetic hormones. I try to believe the bleeding is just part of the purgative process, the toxins pouring out to make me new inside, like the sweat is supposed to do in hot yoga, like a release after a large meal. If I stand up too fast, after an inversion, which I shouldn't do anyway because it worsens my "condition," I sometimes have a big bleed; I tell myself it's just blackberry jam, nothing to fear. The resulting anemia has made me prone to fainting.

I have heard that Christinia is an OB-GYN somewhere in the South, maybe here in Tennessee, an expert in hormonal imbalances. Funny that we both ended up so far from California in some shared ironic reverse migration. Funny that she fixes "feminine problems" now, when she was my problem then. Sometimes I wonder if a black woman I pass in the street is her, if I have unknowingly nodded acknowledgment to or feigned distraction to avoid eye contact with her. When I choose new doctors, I pore over the in-network lists, avoiding Chrissys, Christinias, Christinas. I wonder if I am taking the wrong approach, if somehow only she could tell me what is really wrong with me, could read my body better than a stranger.

. . .

When my head hits the ground, I don't feel the pain at first, just the impact. There's a quick bite and wetness in my mouth, the taste of my own blood, a stranger and a friend at once.

I am struck by the clarity of all things. I see colors more brightly, briefly. I understand. Sometimes the enemy who looks like you is but a preparation for the enemy who is you. The violence directed inside mitigates the violence that comes from outside. It prepares you, creates calluses, fills holes.

The other black woman, the new one, does not have white lint on her feet. I see them up close when she comes—with Biniam and half the class—to see if I'm okay. There are only four black feet, besides mine, in the bunch, so it's easy to recognize hers. Her toenails are painted fuchsia. "I'm a nurse," she says, hovering above me. "Nobody touch her." She checks my airways, shifts my body to Recovery Pose.

The steam and the smell in the room are nauseating. I vomit without my permission. Everyone but her backs away. "Looks like a concussion," the black nurse says. Biniam's feet have disappeared from my line of vision. The woman touches my forehead, my hair, and does not squirm at my sweat on her hand. Moments later, or maybe minutes, I can't be sure, I am lifted by someone— not her, for I can still see her—onto a moving bed.

If the class goes on without me, I will miss Savasana, my favorite part. There is the smell of my own sweat and the bile on my breath and the blood where I bit my tongue. My body has failed me again. Though I have buffeted it, it will not conform. Six months later, after my first of many surgeries, a doctor will pronounce the word "endometriosis" as the cause of all my bleeding.

She will remove the patches and implants that have covered my organs; the chocolate cysts will grow back, again and again. Years later, I will wonder why I competed with that woman in the class, why Christinia competed so much with me. Years later, I will be more informed but no better.

My head and torso are locked in position, but I can still move my fingers and toes. As they carry me to the van, I spread my limbs on the gurney and take my own Savasana. I lie very still, making imperceptible movements in my mind, scanning my body, considering its parts, its defenses, being aware. I recall that I've been doing this yoga since I was a child. I wish I were more evolved.

FATIMA, THE BILOQUIST:
A TRANSFORMATION STORY

There are happier stories one could tell about Fatima. In the nineties you could be whatever you wanted—someone said that on the news—and by 1998 Fatima felt ready to become black, full black, baa baa black sheep black, black like the elbows and knees on praying folk black, if only someone would teach her.

Up to that point she had existed like a sort of colorless gas, or a bit of moisture, leaving the residue of something familiar, sweat stains on a T-shirt, hot breath on the back of a neck, condensation rings on wood, but never a fullness of whatever matter had formed them.

The week she met Violet, Fatima had recited "An Address to the Ladies, by their Best Friend Sincerity" before her eleventh-grade AP English class. She blended her makeup to perfection that morning, but the other students barely looked at her, instead busying themselves by clicking and replacing the lead in mechanical pencils or folding and flicking paper footballs over finger goalposts—even during the part she recited with the most emphasis: "Ah! sad, perverse, degenerate race / The monstrous head deforms the face." They clapped dull palms for a few seconds as Fatima sulked back to her desk. But they sat up, alert, when Wally "The

Wigger" Arnett recited "Incident" and said the word that always made the white kids pay attention.

"You know, I identify with Countee Cullen and all," Wally, with brown freckles and a floppy brown haircut, finished up. "He was a black man, and he was, like, oppressed for who he was and stuff."

The hands pounded a hero's applause as Wally headed back to his seat next to Fatima looking like he expected a high five. She rolled her eyes at him, but she couldn't articulate her wrath into something more specific. Later that morning, when Wally asked her for the fourth time that semester whether she listened to No Limit rappers, she lunged at his face. She had previously tried to explain to Wally, in so many words and dirty looks, that he was not and could not become an honorary black man through his love of Master P. He wore a vague smile that Fatima sometimes read as smug and sometimes as vapid, but he never seemed to hear her. He who would not hear, however, would feel—or would have if Mrs. Bishop hadn't sent Fatima to the principal to "cool down" before her fingernails could scratch off any of Wally's freckles.

It wasn't fair, Fatima thought, that Wally was praised, even mildly popular, for his FUBU shirts and Jordans with the tags still on them, yet Fatima was called "ghetto supastar" the one time she outlined her lips with dark pencil. Nor was it fair that she should get a warning from Principal Lee for "looking like she might become violent" when Wally said "nigger" and got applause. She was still thinking about Wally when she first encountered Violet.

They met at the Montclair Plaza, where Fatima had been dropped off by her mother, Monica, along with the warnings that she better not (1) exceed her allowance of fifty dollars; (2) use her emergency credit card for nonemergencies; or (3) pick up any riffraff, roughnecks, or pregnancies while she was there. Number three was highly unlikely, and Fatima knew Monica knew it, but she said it anyway.

Fatima moped near the Clinique counter with her heavy Discman tucked in a tiny backpack and her headphones wrapped around her neck, trying to decide between one shade of lipstick and another. The college student behind the counter ignored her, chatting with another colleague, and in situations like this, Fatima usually bought something expensive just to show the salesperson that she could. A blond girl with a short bob sauntered up next to her and said, "The burgundy is pretty, but you could do something darker."

Fatima peripherally saw the hair first, so she didn't expect the rest of the package. A voluptuous—really, that was the only word that would work—girl with a wide nose and black features stood next to her. Fatima had a friend with albinism before in preschool who wore thick red glasses and had blushed almost the same color when she wet her pants at naptime once. She recognized in Violet similar features.

"But you could get the same stuff at Claire's for cheaper," Violet said. "It's not like old girl's trying to help you anyway."

The salesgirl, not chastened but amused, moved back to her post and said, "May I help you," in one of those voices that mean "Get lost."

"I'm still—" Fatima started.

But the blond black girl spoke again: "We'd like some free samples of some of the lipsticks, that color"—she pointed, reaching over Fatima to a pot of dark gloss—"and that one."

"We only give samples," the salesgirl said, "to—"

"To everyone who asks, right?" Violet finished.

The sales associate frowned, looked back at her colleague, looked at Violet and Fatima, and frowned again. "I'll get those ready for you," she said.

Fatima considered putting her headphones back on and trying to float out of the department store, away from this loud girl with the jarring features and booming voice.

"Here," Violet said, handing her the dark gloss in its tiny gloss pot.

"You keep it," Fatima said and started trying to vaporize toward the shoe department.

"It's for you," the girl said, following her.

And like that, they were friends, or something to that effect.

. . .

It was Violet's appraisal—"You're, like, totally a white girl, aren't you?"—that set Fatima into motion. They were eating dots of ice cream that same day at the food court after Violet showed Fatima how to get samples from Estée Lauder, Elizabeth Arden, and MAC. Fatima felt a little like a gangster, holding up the reluctant salesgirls for their stash, but she had a nearly full bag of swag by then, perfume, lip gloss, and oil-blotting papers, without spending any of her allowance. It was already too good to be true, so she didn't feel sad when Violet said "white girl," but almost relieved by the inevitable.

Fatima had been accused of whiteness and being a traitor to the race before, whenever she spoke up in Sunday school at her AME church or visited her family in Southeast San Diego (Southeast a universal geographical marker for the ghetto) or when a cute guy who was just about to ask her out backed away, saying,

"You go to private school, don't you?" It was why she didn't have any black friends—and why, she worried, she would never have a boyfriend, even riffraff to upset her mother.

The allegations offended her but never moved her to any action other than private crying or retreating further into her melancholy belief that her school, Westwood Prep, and her parents' high-paying jobs, had made her somehow unfit for black people. Rather than respond, she usually turned up her Discman louder, sinking into the distantly black but presently white sounds of ska and punk, and sang under her breath, "I'm a freak / I'm a freak" (in the style of Silverchair, not Rick James). At the moment she especially enjoyed reading Charles Brockden Brown and daydreaming of a sickly boyfriend like Arthur Mervyn. If black people wouldn't accept her, she would stick to what she knew.

But Violet's judgment held more heft, in her critique a possibility for transformation. When a black girl with natural green eyes and blond hair and a big chest and bubble butt tells you that you, with your sable skin and dark hair, are not black enough, you listen.

"It's not that I'm trying to be white. It's just that's what I'm around."

"You don't have no church friends? You adopted? Your parents white, too?" Violet didn't seem to want a response. "Where do you stay?"

"With my parents." Fatima wondered if something was wrong with Violet for asking such a stupid question.

"I mean where do you live?" Violet asked.

"Upland."

"They got black people there. My cousin Frankie lives there," Violet said, chewing the dots of ice cream in a way that set Fatima's teeth on edge. She wore a tight white top, cream Dickies, and white Adidas tennis shoes.

"Yes, but not on my street." Fatima wore a pink cardigan, black Dickies, and skater shoes, Kastels.

Violet paused her crunching and talking for a moment. "You have a boyfriend?"

Fatima shook her head. "Do you?"

"I'm in between options right now. Anyway, the last one is locked up in Tehachapi."

Fatima nodded. She had a cousin who had served time there. He called her bourgie, and she'd kicked him in the face once, delighting in his fat lip and his inability to hit girls.

"I'm kidding," Violet said. "We don't all get locked up."

Fatima stuttered.

"I can see I'ma have to teach you a lot of things. You ready?" Violet meant ready to leave the food court, but Fatima meant more when she said, "Yeah, I'm ready." And thus began her transformation.

. . .

If only Baratunde Thurston had been writing when Fatima came of age, she could have learned how to be black from a book instead of from Violet's charm school. Even a quick glance at Ralph Ellison could have saved her a lot of trouble, but she wasn't ready for that, caught up, as she was, in the dramas of Arthur Mervyn and Carwin, the Biloquist, and all of them. With Violet's help, Fatima absorbed the sociocultural knowledge she'd missed—not through osmosis or through more relevant literature, but through committed, structured ethnographical study.

She immersed herself in slang as rigorously as she would later immerse herself in Spanish for her foreign-language exam in grad school; she pored over *Vibe* magazine and watched *Yo! MTV Raps* and *The Parkers*, trying to work her mouth around phrases with the same intonation that Countess Vaughn used, a sort of combination of a Jersey accent and a speech impediment. When she couldn't get into those texts, she encouraged herself with the old episodes of *Fresh Prince of Bel-Air* that played in constant early-morning and late-night rotation, feeling assured that if Ashley Banks could, after five seasons, become almost as cool as Will, then she could, too. Her new turns of phrase fit her about as awkwardly as the puffy powder-blue FUBU jacket she found in a thrift store in downtown Rialto.

Still, she was happy when Violet looked approvingly at it. Pale Violet became the arbiter of Fatima's blackness, the purveyor of all things authentic. Though she was five feet eight and chunky by most standards—nearly obese by Fatima's—you would think Violet, judging by the way she walked, was Pamela Anderson, like a hula doll on a dashboard swinging hips and breasts.

The distance between their respective houses was fifteen minutes, but only seven if they met halfway, Fatima borrowing her father's extra car (the 1993 Beamer, so as not to look ostentatious) and Violet getting a ride from one of her brothers or occasionally driving her mother's old Taurus. They never met at each other's houses, lest Fatima's upper-middle opulence embarrass Violet, and because there was no space for Violet to carve out for herself at her house.

Violet made Fatima a study guide of the top ten black expressions for rating attractive men, and they practiced the pronunciations together. The pinnacle of hotness, according to Violet, was either "dangfoine," "hella foine, or "bout it, bout it," as in "Oooh, he bout it, bout it." This phrase especially required the Countess Vaughn intonation and often included spontaneous bouts of raising the roof.

During their tutoring sessions, Fatima stifled her joke about the rain in Spain falling mostly on the plains and practiced on, assured that Violet's instruction would confer upon her, like Carwin, "a wonderful gift" of biloquism.

Glossaries soon followed, in which Violet broke down slang that had previously mystified Fatima. She couldn't wait to replace her traditional "fer shure" with "fisshow" in a real conversation, but she took issue with some of Violet's recommendations, especially "nigga" and "gangsta," which Violet explained as terms of endearment. "So basically," Fatima summarized, ventriloquizing Ashley Banks again, "you want me to turn good things into bad things and vice versa."

Violet said, "Mostly."

Fatima tried pumping her shoulders in a brief Bankhead Bounce, but it was obvious she lacked the follow-through and wasn't ready for dancing yet.

And it was almost like any romantic comedy in which the sassy black person moves in with the white people and teaches them how to live their lives in color and put some bass in their voices, only Steve Martin wasn't in it, and no one was a maid or a butler or nanny, and the romance was between two girls, and it was platonic, and they were both black this time, but one didn't look like it, and one didn't sound like it, at least not consistently.

· · ·

"They racist up at that school? I can't stand cocky white people," Violet said one day while they sat at their usual table, near the flower divider in the mall's arboretum. Some white guys from Hillwood sat across the way, laughing loudly.

Fatima didn't like to talk about her school, but everyone in the Inland Empire knew Westwood and Hillwood, rivals on and off the football field. "I don't think so," Fatima said.

"What do you mean you don't think so? Either something's racist or it's not."

No one at school poked out his tongue and called her *that*, like they did in the poem Wally read, but Fatima thought about Wally, his affectations, and Principal Lee.

"It's not always comfortable," she said. "It can be awkward, but I'm awkward."

"You sure are." Violet laughed, and Fatima laughed, too. She was learning to do more of that, and to wear a kind of self-assuredness with her side-swooped Aaliyah bangs.

In fact, most interactions were easier with Violet than they were with others. Violet understood things. Fatima never had to explain why she might wrap her hair in a silk scarf at bedtime or why she always carried a tube of hand cream to prevent not only chapped hands, but also allover ashiness. Those shared practices validated Fatima, and so did Violet's understanding of Fatima's fears about her body. "Sometimes I just feel horrible about all of it, the sweating, the bleeding. I don't always feel like a regular girl, you know?" Fatima said one day, "But what is normal anyway?"

"Word, that's deep," Violet said, and explained that she, too, felt the weight of her body, because it did not look "like what people expect black to be." In spite of her seeming confidence, Violet confided, she had a complex about her albinism. Fatima understood when Violet intimated that albinism marked her as both desirable for her lightness, her hair color, her eye color, and yet despised for some perceived physical untruth. Fatima had seen the way people glanced two and three times at Violet, deciding where to place her and whether she warranted any of the benefits of whiteness. Violet could call other black people like Fatima white, but to be called white herself pushed Violet to violent tears. Just ask her ex-boyfriend and her ex-friend Kandice from middle school, who had called her Patti Mayonnaise in a fit of anger and gotten a beatdown that made her wet her pants like Fatima's preschool friend.

"Why Patti Mayonnaise?" Fatima said.

"You know, from *Doug*, she was the black girl on the DL who looked white, and mayonnaise is white. It's a stupid joke."

"Patti was black?" Fatima said.

"Girl, a whole lot of everybody got black in them," Violet started.

Fatima had heard some of Violet's theories before during a game they sometimes played on the phone. The list included Jennifer Beals, Mariah Carey, and "that freaky girl from *Wild Things*," Denise Richards, and now, apparently, Patti Mayonnaise. When Fatima suggested Justin Timberlake, Violet said, "Nah, he's like that Wally kid at your school."

The nuances of these and other things Emily, Fatima's best friend since second grade, just couldn't understand, no matter how earnestly she tried or how many questions she asked, like why they couldn't share shampoo when she slept over, or "What does 'For us, by us' even mean," and why Fatima's top lip was darker than her bottom one.

Fatima picked up some theories on her own, too, without Violet or the literature. The thing about the brown top lip and the pink lower one, Fatima had pieced together after what she learned from Violet and what she had learned at school, was that you could either read them as two souls trying to merge into a better self, or you could conceal them under makeup and talk with whichever lip was convenient for the occasion. At school and with Emily, she talked with her pink lip, and with Violet, she talked with her brown one, and that created tension only if she thought too much about it.

. . .

Fatima passed the time at school by imagining the time she would spend after school with Violet, who promised to teach her how to flirt better on their next excursion and to possibly, eventually, hook her up with one of her cousins, but not one of her brothers, because "Most of them aren't good for anything except upsetting your mother, if you want to do that." Fatima did not want to do that.

Now at school when Wally the Wigger looked like he was even thinking about saying something to her, Fatima made a face that warned, "Don't even look like you're thinking about saying something to me," and he obeyed. In her mind, she not only said this aloud, but said it in Violet's voice.

She didn't mind the laughter in her parents' eyes when she tried out a new phrase or hairstyle, because it was all working. There was something prettier about her now, too, and people seemed to see it before Fatima did, because a guy named Rolf at Westwood—a tall brunette in her history class, with whom she'd exchanged a few eye rolls over Wally—asked her for her phone number.

Without pausing to consider anything, she gave it to him.

IT MIGHT SEEM, up to this point, that Fatima simultaneously wore braces, glasses, and forehead acne, when you hardly needed to glance to see the gloss of her black hair or the sheen on her shins, with or without lotion. Fatima knew this truth instinctively, but buried its warmth under the shame of early-childhood teasing and a preference for melancholy self-pity. It was more romantic to feel ugly than to pretend she couldn't hold her head just right, unleash her beautiful teeth, and make a skeptical man kneel at her skirt's hem. She just didn't have the practice, but she was hopeful that she might get it, with Rolf or one of Violet's cousins, hopeful that the transformation had taken hold.

. . .

She had just returned from a movie with Violet—where not one but two guys had asked for her phone number, though three had asked for Violet's, pronouncing their approval of her "thickness" with grunts, smiles, and by looking directly at her butt—when her mother said, "You got a phone call, from a boy."

It couldn't be one of the boys from the theater already; that would make anyone look desperate.

"Who is Rolf?" her mother asked with a smile, "and why didn't you mention him before?"

Fatima nearly floated up to her bedroom. She thought about calling Violet but called Rolf back instead, waiting, of course, for an hour to pass, a tip she had learned from Violet in the event of a hypothetical situation such as this.

By now, and with some authenticity, Fatima could intone the accent marks in places they hadn't been before, recite all the names of all the members of Cash Money, Bad Boy, No Limit, Wu-Tang, Boyz II Men, ABC, BBD, ODB, LDB, TLC, B-I-G-P-O-P-P-A, Ronny, Bobby, Ricky, Mike, Ralph, Johnny, Tony, Toni, and Tone, if she wanted. But when she called Rolf, all they talked about were skateboards and the Smiths, in whose music Fatima had dabbled before Violet.

"The Smiths are way better than Morrissey," Rolf said. His voice was nasal but deep.

"You can barely tell the difference since Morrissey's voice is so overpowering," she said, from her pink lip.

"No, but the Smiths' stuff is way darker," Rolf said. "You should hear the first album. Then you'll get it. I've got it on vinyl."

"Okay," Fatima waited.

She noticed that he didn't invite her over to listen or offer to lend her the album, but he did call back two days later and ask if she wanted to hang out over the next weekend, "like at the mall or something, see a movie?"

Fatima counted to twelve, as per the rules (the universal ones, not just Violet's) and said, "Yeah, that'd be cool." She almost left the "l" off the end of the word, but caught herself. "Which mall?"

"Where else?" Rolf said. "The Montclair Plaza."

This would be her first date, and though that was the kind of thing to share with a best friend, especially one with more experience, Fatima felt—in some deep way that hurt her stomach—that Violet didn't need to know about Rolf, not yet at least. She would keep her lips glossed and parted, her two worlds separate.

· · ·

The week leading up to the first date, Fatima tried to play extra-cool, asking Violet more questions than usual when they spoke on the phone. Neither of the guys from the movie theater had called Fatima, but one of Violet's three had asked Violet out, and she was "letting him stew for a while before I let him know. Anyway, I thought you wanted to check out *Rush Hour* this weekend."

"This weekend?" Fatima said.

"This weekend."

"I told my parents I would babysit this weekend, I forgot," Fatima lied, feeling a bit like a grease stain on a silk shirt.

"Since when?" Violet pushed.

"We can go next weekend, or during the week," Fatima said, and changed the subject.

Before they got off the phone, Violet said, "I guess I'll call Mike back, then, and tell him I'm free after all."

. . .

Fatima would say that she wasn't embarrassed by Violet or Rolf, but she wasn't ready for them to meet. She felt relief, then, when their first and second dates went without a hitch—and ended with a gentle but sort of indifferent kiss—and even more relieved that Rolf was okay with seeing each other during the week so that Fatima wouldn't have to explain to Violet why she suddenly had other plans on Friday and Saturday evenings.

"Tell me more about your other friends," Rolf had said on the phone one night, when Fatima was starting to think she might love him. He knew Emily from school. He knew she went to an AME church.

He'd met her parents and siblings by then, though she still hadn't met his. When he first came over to the house, he shook hands with Fatima's father—noting Mr. Willis's height with a "Whoa, you're tall"—and hugged her mother and patted her six-year-old brother's head awkwardly, in a way that reminded Fatima of someone stroking a rabbit's foot for luck.

At dinner Rolf chatted to excess, complimenting the drapes, the silverware, and Fatima's frowny-faced eight-year-old sister and indifferent younger brother. She wasn't sure how nervous either of them should be. She found his foot with hers under the table and smiled silently, "Calm down. Be quiet." She tried to signal, but Rolf prattled on, "I think it's great that you as a black family are so successful."

No one addressed Rolf, but her parents stood to clear the dishes. She heard their irritation in faint whispers from the kitchen, could see it in their eyes even with their backs turned. Fatima declined dessert. "We have to get to the movies. We'll get some candy there," she said.

Still, she and Rolf were together a month later, and her parents hadn't expressed any concrete disapproval. A month later, she was only just telling Rolf about Violet.

"I guess my other best friend," Fatima responded, "besides Emily, is Violet."

"Violet," Rolf repeated. "Cool name. She's not at Westwood, is she?"

"No, public school."

"Ah," Rolf said, in a tone that Fatima interpreted as neutral.

"She's my girl." She stopped herself from saying "Ace boon coon." "We hang out a lot on the weekends, actually."

"How come you never mentioned her before?"

"I don't know." Fatima felt her mouth lying again, moving somehow separately from her real voice. "She's kind of shy. She got teased a lot."

"Oh, that's too bad," Rolf said.

"They called her Patti Mayonnaise," Fatima said, and she didn't know why it was she who was now prattling on.

"Don't tell anybody this, but I always thought Patty was cute on *Doug*," Rolf said, and shifted to talking about all his favorite cartoons. Fatima exhaled.

. . .

Over time they grew to joke, a little awkwardly, about Fatima's position at school, as one of two black girls. She asked Rolf if this was a thing for him or if she was his first black girlfriend, because by now they called each other boyfriend and girlfriend.

"I don't see color," he said. "I just saw you. Like, one day there you were."

Violet would have said that color-blind people were the same ones who followed you in the store and that Rolf's game was hella corny.

"Anyway, it's not like you're black black," Rolf said.

Fatima remembered the lifelessness, before Violet, of feeling like a colorless gas and tried, in spite of a dull ache and the numbness of her brown lip, to take Rolf's words as a compliment.

. . .

The conventions of such a transformation dictate that a snaggletooth or broken heel threatens to return the heroine to her former life. That snaggletooth, for Fatima, was either Rolf or Violet, depending on how you looked at things, and Fatima wasn't sure how she did.

When she saw Violet, on April 4—after hiding her relationship with Rolf for three months—approaching from across the lobby of Edwards Cinema with Mike's arm around her waist, Fatima's first instinct was to grab Rolf's hand and steer him toward the exit. But Violet was already calling her name.

This wasn't the natural order of things, for these separate lives to converge. Other factors aside, the code went hos before bros, school life before social life, family before anyone else. But Rolf was both school and social, and Violet both social and nearly family, and Fatima's math skills couldn't balance this equation.

"I knew I saw you," Violet said to Fatima once she got close. "Who is this?"

"Rolf, Violet. Violet, Rolf," Fatima said, "and Mike."

Mike smiled, and Rolf smiled, and they shook hands, but neither young woman saw the guys, their eyes deadlocked on each other.

"Ha, so this is Violet," Rolf said, ignoring or misreading Fatima's firm grip on his arm. "Even your black friends are white, too." Rolf laughed.

"I was gonna tell you—" Fatima started to say to Violet.

"Wait, Patti Mayonnaise, I get it now," Rolf said aloud, then, "Oops, I—" and both women scowled at him.

Fatima made a noise that could be interpreted as either a guffaw or a deep moan.

When she turned back to Violet, though she opened and closed her mouth several times, no sounds emerged. She didn't mean to hurt her; some things had just come out, and other things she hadn't told Violet because she wasn't sure which lip she was supposed to use. Before she knew it, her voice was over there and then over there, and she was ventriloquizing what she'd learned all at once, but from too many places and all at the wrong time.

Violet didn't curse or buck up as though she might hit Fatima— though perhaps one of those options might have been better; she just grabbed Mike's arm and walked away.

And like that, Fatima was a vapor again, but something darker, like a funnel cloud, or black smoke that mocked what was already singed.

THE SUBJECT OF CONSUMPTION

No one had come right out and said it, but Mike intuited that he might never advance past this stage in his career. The rule was that you couldn't go backward. Whatever baseline he established with the first show could curve only upward, never down. If he'd started with, say, some original series about dating with disabilities and sold it as straight realism, he could do what he wanted now. But since he started with filth, he could get only grittier. The people were always hungry, the viewers and the "talent," as they called the fame whores; they were downright gluttonous. Mike wanted to shift toward ironic documentaries with a sharp lens, but who would respect the artistry of the man who brought the world such jewels as *Pet Psychics of Rhode Island* and *My Big Fat Gay Dads*? So, here he was, at the house, heaping muck upon muck in order to form a more perfect dross pile.

The neighborhood's landscape belied the inner contents of the house. Oak and spruce trees stretched over Tudor roofs and lawns so smooth they looked vacuumed; women in gardening hats bent over patches of flowers gradated by height; lawn tools filled truck beds. Mike had pitched his first two series for the network—one on a set of twin sisters married to the same man and one on a pair of married white pastors raising ten adopted black children—with similar "behind these walls" premises. Mike's use of cutaways from outside to inside—from the family looking suburban in the front yard, to the real workings of the house—attracted indignant viewers who couldn't believe anyone lived this way. One of the sister-wife twins had stumbled across the blog of Lisbeth Hoag and tipped Mike off to this family he was preparing to shoot.

"We'll set up across the street for the long shots of the house, and then you'll set up again in the driveway and come in close on the family." Mike flattened the collar on his fitted pink polo shirt and walked up the drive toward the front door. A few men in jeans and Dickies began unloading cameras and stands from the van, the large man with the boom watching awkwardly, not really helping anyone.

Before Mike could ring the doorbell, Lisbeth opened the red oversize door, a mismatch for the otherwise English architecture, and told him to come in.

"Liz. Good to see you. So we're setting up outside, for now. Where's the family?"

Mike had gotten used to Lisbeth's appearance and the appearance of the inner house after their first few meetings. Her small frame was all angles and melasmic patches of skin, the missing tooth jarring, yet she might have been pretty at some point. He made a mental note to ask for pictures of her younger self.

Inside, the house at 406 Wedgewood was immaculately organized but felt almost third world if not vaguely tropical. Each of the three times he'd previously visited to talk about the pilot, the smell—a mix of sulfuric eggs and perspiration—had overwhelmed Mike before he saw its source. Eighteen-quart storage tubs of bananas, young coconuts, mangoes, tomatoes, and durians sat in a neat row along the perimeter of the kitchen, each fruit type separated into its own tub, the durians' essence overpowering the freshness of the other food and permeating the few pieces of furniture. Mike wondered how the lighting guys could best capture the gnats and vinegar flies surrounding the tubs. Each common room included bookcases and at least one papasan chair, but there were no couches. A couple of twin mattresses without frames lined the floors of two of the three bedrooms; the mattresses, covered with gray-green and navy blue sheets, seemed to absorb the smell of the durians as well.

"They got the schedule, but they're out, actually," Lisbeth said, and Mike sensed irritation in her voice. "Ryan's not answering his phone, but knowing him, he probably lost it."

"Out," Mike repeated, running through possible revisions that wouldn't waste the daylight needed for the exterior shots with the whole family. He'd already stressed in his phone calls and emails the importance of call times and the tightness of the schedule. "Okay," he started. A better director would have pried for more information about Ryan's silence. Were the marital problems escalating? Maybe he should get Lisbeth to say that again on camera. The story arc should show the lifestyle's strain on the family.

"I was thinking we could rearrange the shooting schedule and you could get some footage of me working on the blog or in the back gardens," Lisbeth said, walking him through the kitchen to the family room but offering him no place to sit.

Mike didn't like it when the talent tried to direct, even if she had a point. "When do you think Ryan and Inedia will be back?" he asked, shaking his hand no at the maca-matcha tea Lisbeth offered.

"I don't know," Lisbeth said, flicking a matted blond dread over her shoulder. "I could talk more about the lifestyle. Why can't we just shoot me?"

He couldn't put his finger on what Lisbeth reminded him of, but he could use that sound bite for all kinds of things; a crescendo, for instance: "Why don't you just shoot me? Just shoot me. Shoot me."

. . .

"Please, Daddy." Ryan paused to look warningly at Inedia, who pointed to a bright blue sleeping bag with Disney characters printed on it. "I mean, Ryan," she self-corrected. "Could we get this one?"

Her quiet begging seemed muffled among the voices of shrieking, crying, or otherwise noisy children in Walmart as Inedia's eyes darted around the warehouse, taking in the colors. The lights buzzed in Ryan's ears, punctuated the grinding sensation around the right side of his forehead, loosening teeth from his jaws. His prana hurt.

Ryan had given up on his search for a used children's sleeping bag after the fourth thrift store, on the other side of town, produced no results. Probably because even thrift stores wouldn't take dingy used sleeping bags stained with child's pee and drool. A bag from Walmart or any other big-box store—he imagined Lisbeth lecturing—sent the wrong message, as did Snow White, Elsa, and any other Disney princess who came in a full line of pastel products, but at least the sleeping bag would be clean.

He shook his head, not looking at Inedia, but at the large cage-like display of children's sleeping bags. He pointed to his left, where the utilitarian bags were stacked, and touched the fabric of a gray adult-size bag. The adult bag cost $49.95; Elsa, $14.99. The adult bag was weatherproofed and down filled; Elsa, flimsy and filled with synthetics.

. . .

"This one," he said, pointing again to the gray bag, though it pained him to pay extra for a bag they needed only for show.

Inedia didn't cry like most kids would, and there was something about her lack of reaction that made Ryan both angry and sympathetic. He had not set out to be subversive that morning, to miss his call time while scouring Goodwills from El Camino to Santa Cruz only to end up at Walmart, but he was here now. Lisbeth would already be mad. Mike was really missing out, he thought, by not capturing this.

FUELED BY A surge of spontaneity, he placed the Elsa bag into their basket and felt a small sense of fulfillment. He could make choices, too; she was his daughter, too.

"Thank you, Ryan." Inedia barely smiled. She had a way of doing that, of not reacting the way he expected her to. When she was a few months old, before Lisbeth had gotten the fellowship that took them to Costa Rica, he'd pinched Inedia's arm a little as she sat in one of those sit-up baby chairs, just to see what would happen. She didn't cry. She looked at him, rocking herself in her footed onesie forward with her legs and back, and matched his gaze for a while, as if saying, "I understand."

An old man stared into Ryan's face and then Inedia's before he shuffled away, mumbling "Cute kid." Regardless of which parent took her out (though it was usually Ryan), people stared at Inedia, equally interested in her sharp contrast to her father's deep brown as in her softer sable to Lisbeth's pinkness. Ryan took Inedia's hand. He craved pineapple, something acidic and stinging to cleanse his mouth. Lisbeth wouldn't approve of the purchase from this store. To get to the fruit section, he cut across from the camping gear, past the fishing poles, the smell of chicken-blood bait sitting heavy in his nostrils. The fishing aisle gave way to the craft and sewing sections, which led, after the small city of baby products, to a quick detour through the beverage aisles and eventually a straight line to the produce. For all his resistance to Walmart, he didn't want to go home.

. . .

"As you can see, these tubs are well organized, and all the fruit is fresh," Lisbeth said facing the camera, walking the crew to the container of mangoes. She smelled one and overemoted its visible ripeness. "That life-giving flesh; there's strong prana in living food. You can absorb it through the third eye. Can you bring the boom in closer?" She looked above the camera to the large man, who looked at Mike. "I don't like to raise my voice."

"Talk a little about your process for prepping meals," Mike said, feeling a headache building at his temples. "What do you do with all the durian?"

"So we store the fruit in these tubs, and we also use them as sorts of troughs to eat from. Ryan and Inedia make a big batch of whatever we're eating, say, durian pudding, mango salsa, or tomato with avocado and lemon, early in the morning. And then we graze from the tubs all day. Fruitarians have to eat a lot to stay full." Lisbeth patted her nonexistent paunch for emphasis.

Mike motioned for the cameraman, Jonathan, to come in for a medium shot that would show Lisbeth's missing back tooth.

"It sounds like a lot of food," she continued, "but it goes right through you. We—well, Ryan actually—does the shopping twice a week. We buy crates directly from the farmers at the farmers' market or from organic grocers we've built relationships with. We harvest our own avocados and the maca out back," she said, pointing to the screen doors. "It's Inedia's job to organize and wash the fruit with a white vinegar solution."

"What do you do?" Mike said from off camera.

"I manage it all, and I run our blogs and vlogs." With each hand, Lisbeth twirled a thick dread in contrasting directions, like some kind of double dutch tic, or as if the hair were saying *"Muy loca."* "I'm more the philosophy behind the practice," she said, letting the hair fall.

Mike wasn't sure if he could stand a whole day of filming with her alone. "Why don't we have you sit in one of the papasan chairs and shoot some confession-cam footage? Talk about the bed situation, in the present tense." It was hard to set up the shots so that they both accentuated and blurred Lisbeth's skin. You couldn't let all the ugly cracks and spots show on camera, or no one would watch; too clean, though, and the realness of the thing would be minimized.

"Oh, sure."

· · ·

This was Ryan's first time at Walmart in a year or so. They'd started buying the toilet paper in bulk there after the first two months of the transition, but they didn't need as much now. Before

Inedia was born, Ryan and Lisbeth had each gone through a roll a day, dabbing at the liquid tar the online community had warned them about. There had been so many lifestyle experiments with Lisbeth: from ayurvedic eating based on their individual doshas to macrobiotic to vegan to raw. The groceries became more expensive and the lifestyle more time-consuming the closer they tried to get to earth, to original man, to whatever: ceramic knives instead of metal ones—to prevent oxidization—glassware and BPA-free everything, not that there were ever leftovers.

Looking back on his decision, Ryan must have been hungry when he agreed to quit his job to manage Lisbeth's Web presence and "fully commit to the lifestyle." It certainly didn't make sense. The former financial planner in him couldn't always look away. If the mortgage hadn't been paid by Lisbeth's father's estate, they wouldn't have been able to afford it for the food. They had blown through what was left of Ryan's investments on the first failed durian distribution business, and the compost wasn't making much money, but the YouTube channels were picking up subscribers and ad revenue, enough to pay for groceries each week, enough to attract Mike and the network.

After the transition to fruitarian, they continued to buy the cheap toilet paper because even Lisbeth agreed that the recycled bamboo stuff was too expensive. The toilet paper, and the diapers after Inedia was born, were the only things Lisbeth would allow Ryan to buy from a big-box store that, she said, traded in child or third-world labor and that stood for some kind of capitalistic, imperialistic, or otherwise -istic enterprises. Technically and ethically, they were supposed to use cloth diapers, but Lisbeth said, "The solvents and energy used to launder the diapers, even with a cleaning service, are way worse for the earth than tossing the diapers." She said something about putting compost back into the earth this way.

Ryan had enjoyed the shopping less since Lisbeth started double- and triple-checking the labels and the receipts. Still, there was something comforting about the expansive space of a Walmart, despite the unrelenting brightness: the sight of an old woman with a heavy lipstick line drawn just above the vermillion border bouncing an orange in her hand or squeezing a melon for firmness, the heavy, genetically modified cotton shirts and sweatpants that came in extra-large sizes, the rows of colorful school supplies and greeting cards printed with animal-tested inks and artificial dyes.

So today, the trip to Walmart felt just as right as the *Frozen*-branded sleeping bag in their shopping cart. Lisbeth would want a point-by-point summary of their excursion, but she'd pantomime for the cameras, wait until the crew left to explode. He pulled Inedia out of the self-checkout line, the sleeping bag and pineapple still in the cart, and retreated back into the comfort of the crowd. "Let's look at the toy aisle," he said to Inedia.

· · ·

Per Mike's direction, Lisbeth pretended to spell-check the post before pushing Submit and flipping through her handwritten notes for ideas for Wednesday's installment. She read some of the ideas aloud directly to the camera, then explained that the blog had picked up a lot of traffic ever since she'd started including pictures of Inedia and the neighborhood, as if the images crystallized the rhetoric.

She stared at the man behind the camera in a way that Mike read as flirtatious before continuing, "When he first started formatting the website, Ryan was always whining that he and Inedia should have been in the picture, too, to emphasize the familial part. But I said, 'As the principal researcher and author, I don't think I should undermine my credibility with a traditional Western hausfrau picture.' Now he doesn't even want to be on the site—or in this show," she said, lowering her voice.

"Talk more about that," Mike stalled.

"Well, the blog was Ryan's idea, but you would never know it. I had come home crying after a meeting with my dissertation adviser. After I passed my orals, she said she thought I should seek a new direction. Whatever. The IRB—this review board that makes sure you're doing ethical research—wouldn't approve of the project. So Ryan suggested that I choose a different official research project and keep my interests in detachment parenting alive in some other form; hence the blog and the vlog."

She continued, "We're like our own focus group. Inedia takes agency over her homeschooling, and she's good—for a seven-year-old, she's good. Ryan does the Web design, shopping, food prep, deals with the produce vendors. I told you about the harvesting."

"You did," Mike said, realizing that he was sweating. "Tell us about some of the stuff you put on the websites and people's responses to it."

They shot an hour and a half of footage of Lisbeth reenacting responses to comments on her various Internet platforms. She was not a good actress. She tried to squeeze out a tear as she recounted the "many, many people" who asked how any self-respecting upper-middle-class family could live like this. Mike still couldn't pinpoint who she reminded him of, someone weather-beaten and frazzled. The tearfulness seemed insincere, but when Lisbeth cursed the entire child-welfare system of Palo Alto and Northern California more generally, her anger was genuine.

"I swear it was Alice Faye, two houses down, who made the phone call," Lisbeth said, looking past the cameras and directly at Mike. "That was after the first time Inedia ran off and they found her in the neighbor's yard eating grass. I could have made her a green juice if I had known her body needed the chlorophyll."

Mike shot a look at the crew member who'd elbowed him. With his eyes, he said, "Just humor her for a minute." He didn't tell Lisbeth that they would incorporate content from the blog later, that her computer screen would interfere with the camera, making wavy lines; he let her keep talking for a while before asking her to try Ryan's phone again.

. . .

With the *Frozen* sleeping bag, the pineapple, and now a trinket for Inedia in his hands, Ryan and Inedia made their way back toward the registers. The self-check line was short but barely moved as customers struggled to find bar codes or as the machine told them to "please place the item back in the bagging area" and to "wait for the attendant." Ryan thought what a spectacle it all was, how Lisbeth would criticize him for returning home with not only an Elsa bag, but one from Walmart, for his own kid, whom he took care of better than she did.

"Inedia," he said—and realizing the unkemptness of her black curls, the crusty smear of something orange near her chin, he felt self-conscious—"don't tell Liz where we got this, okay?"

"Okay," she said, playing with a box of pink Tic Tacs.

"It'll be our secret, like the others." He nodded with her, almost wishing he could buy her some candy, something king-size and chocolate, but that would add to the number of secrets, not conceal it.

A woman in front of them, black and middle-aged, turned around and looked Ryan over, judgmentally, he thought. Then, still half turned to him, she said to Inedia, "That's a pretty sleeping bag, sweetie. You going to a sleepover or camping?"

Inedia became more sullen when strangers spoke to her. She put down the mints and looked at Ryan as if for permission to speak, then said, "No."

"Well, what's it for, then, sweetie?"

"To sleep in."

The woman hesitated for a second, looked back at Ryan, holding a definite glare, and said, "Hmm," before turning around in line.

In truth, Inedia slept in one of the twin beds, with a matching bamboo sheet set and comforter, but Lisbeth wanted to strip the beds bare to corroborate her claims about the family's nomadic Romani-style living—though Ryan didn't think the Romani even lived that way. And, she speculated, "The more skeletal the house looks, the more likely they are to do a crossover episode with one of the network's home makeover shows. We could get a whole new interior for free."

They could get a whole new interior for free by paying to make their current interior look worse, reverse house-staging—it didn't make sense to Ryan. Inedia's bed, according to Lisbeth, needed the sleeping bag, an old one, to pull the look together.

The woman glanced at Inedia and Ryan again before paying for her groceries. Ryan knew some black women judged him for choosing Lisbeth. He had heard his mother's and sisters' and college friends' appraisals of black men who dated white and could even understand the accusations that some black men chose "any old white woman," as his first college girlfriend, Jessie, had put it. "I mean, she could be toothless, big as a house, and speaking the fakest-sounding Ebonics you could imagine, and they'll jump over four highly educated black women to hold the door for a bowser, just to have little light-skinned babies with her."

Lisbeth wasn't a bowser, originally. She had been beautiful once—an eight—with a kind of hard-line assertiveness that still felt soft. They met at UC Berkeley under a tree to which several students had chained themselves. They both skated up on their respective boards, Lisbeth's a longboard and Ryan's a skateboard, and paused to see the commotion. Protests were a daily occurrence, and neither could remember what this protest was about, only that their eyes met and that they both laughed at the hippies in the tree. Lisbeth wore little Capri Sun straws in her earlobes, which, she explained, she was stretching. Her top, simple and black, paired with jean shorts, accentuated her breasts, uncontained by a bra. She complimented Ryan's short dreads. Their relationship developed quickly, the sex intense, and Ryan could almost drown out the judgment and Jessie's theory that Lisbeth was just trying to make her parents mad. When Lisbeth was assaulted near campus their senior year, Ryan became her sole source of support, which initially had a damaging effect. They broke up briefly, Lisbeth claiming, "I don't like how dependent I feel when I'm with you." But they reunited, spent happy years traveling, making plans, eventually settling, with some recognition of the irony, into their own hippie comforts, the stability of Ryan's income, and the softness of each other.

He loved her, but increasingly Lisbeth scared Ryan. He had watched his father, a businessman, take care of his schizophrenic mother, who on lucid days made artwork that hung in galleries from Riverside to Cape Cod. On bad days, she went missing for weeks at a time, leaving no food in the fridge. Ryan's dad would return home, comfort the kids with expensive toys and fast food, and go back to work. His mother was institutionalized four times during his childhood before her suicide when Ryan was sixteen.

Lisbeth never went missing, but her shrinking frame and increasing delusions were a kind of disappearing, too, a propulsion toward death. Ryan couldn't pinpoint when the days began to slow down, when Lisbeth became an embarrassment, the flint of her shrinking body a bone against his own.

. . .

The introduction on the blog's welcome page featured a picture of Lisbeth with fuller cheeks and a peachy glow on her skin, unlike the sallow, patchy face in front of Mike and the camera. She stood next to a tree, wearing a blue tank top, holding a durian, and smiling.

The note on the webpage read in part:

Detachment parenting works from the premise that early peoples had it right and babies and children were essentially adults in miniature. If left to perform tasks on their own, they will develop useful skills and become self-sufficient.

Lisbeth told the cameras, "I don't believe in all that smothering my parents did to me, stuffing me into puffy dresses and making me their world. It's so suffocating. We were wrong to name our daughter Inedia. At first—I think I had postpartum because I didn't encapsulate my placenta—I was all into the idea that she'd be our sole source of prana, our air, that we could draw everything from her. But the more I read about the benefits of the lifestyle, and the more I got in touch with the food, the more I realized that we should have named her something empowering for her and for us."

Mike nodded, hoping the condescension didn't show.

"We're thinking of changing her name to Busela or something more independent."

"You'd change a child's name at seven?"

Lisbeth was doing that thing with her hair again. "We waited ten days before her Namakarma Sanskar ceremony as it was; we believe in the traditional way, that a name should reflect the character."

"And this is the kind of stuff you put on the website?" Mike moved his hand to suggest she should elaborate.

Links to previous installments of the blog appeared in the sidebar, listed in chronological order. Lisbeth named them and told anecdotes about each:

October 19: Breastfeeding: A Lot like Cannibalism, No?
October 26: Breastfeeding, Part Two: Baby Vampirism: Let
    Them Suck the Life Out of You If You Want
November 2: Elimination Anticipation
November 9: Solutions for Accidental Elimination
November 16: Cold Bath, No Colic

Among the links listed under "Resources" were websites from which readers could purchase tiny underwear made specially for children under age one, imported infant toilet seats, colorless handmade wooden toys, and links to her fruitarian lifestyle pages and family vlogs, respectively.

This stuff could really work, Mike thought, but they needed Inedia, Bucolic, or whatever the child's name would be, and Ryan. Lisbeth on her own was insufferable.

. . .

In the Walmart parking lot, Ryan removed the sticker from the pineapple and stuck it, once he got it off his finger, inside his pocket. He unzipped the thick plastic that held the sleeping bag and handed it to Inedia. He separated the cardboard from the clamshell Polly Pocket case and handed the trash to his daughter. "Throw all this away over there." When she returned from the trash can, a few cars away from theirs, he was stepping on the bag, grinding in a little oil with the toe of his boot. "Jump on," he directed Inedia. She followed, trying to rub the bag with the dirt on the bottom of her scuffed Crocs. They would wash and dry the bag when they got home, to make the stains look set.

"Kinda fun, isn't it?"

Inedia nodded.

When the bag was sufficiently stained, Ryan rolled it up and secured the roll with the two blue elastic straps attached to the bag. He tucked it in the back seat of the car, next to Inedia's booster seat, and signaled to make the left turn toward home, but made a sharp right instead. In the rearview mirror, he saw Inedia clutching her new toy awkwardly, as if she didn't know what to do with such a sophisticated object—in contrast to the monochrome wooden toys Lisbeth gave her—with so many tiny pieces.

"You hungry?"

Inedia smiled for the first time that day. "Yes."

Inedia had been a small baby, her cheeks and the spaces around her eyes thin and bluish even now under her glasses. She was only two weeks early, but because Lisbeth was so thin, the doctor said, the baby did not have much to work with. They stayed in the hospital while they fed mother and child with an IV. Lisbeth had protested that she was "not malnourished, you imbeciles," and that the IV "had better be supplied by plant-based sources," or she might sue. After two weeks, they let her out, and a week later they let Inedia leave, but not before Dr. Sun warned that he would call child services if Inedia did not gain weight by her six-week checkup. At seven, Inedia still sat in a booster seat, partly because of the laws in California, and partly because she could never catch up to other kids in height any better than Ryan or Lisbeth could maintain weight.

He parked at McDonald's and went around to help Inedia out of the back seat.

"We're going to eat here?"

"We're going to eat here."

. . .

Mike held his hand to one temple as Lisbeth went on and on about how she'd come to realize that the blog market was all about getting people to argue. She was right that the television series would work the same way if the cable network picked it up. The blog's popularity seemed only to reassure Lisbeth of her expertise. Over a lunch of cold tomato-and-tomato sandwiches, she rehearsed for Mike, who had let the crew take thirty, her plans to self-publish an e-book that would "get my work out there to more people."

"I know what you're thinking," she said, tilting her head from side to side, "but it has nothing to do with the profit." She looked

at him. "We don't usually eat nuts—cashews aren't even technically raw because of the extraction process—but Ryan thought
you'd like something more substantial." She handed him a plate.

Mike spread a thin layer of the cashew cheese over a slice of
tomato and tried not to look up at Lisbeth. The vapors from the
durian gas had given him something like a buzz.

"And how do you make enough to live here anyway?"

"Oh, our parents helped us a bit. Ryan's family—before his
parents died—were capitalists, but they never made any real
money. Mine—well, my mom; my dad's dead, too—is still a capi-
talist. I don't have a problem with taking the money or the profits
from the blog because we're redistributing it into sustainability.
The produce we buy sends the money right back into the hands of
the local grower. We sell the composted material to some of the
neighbors and one farmer. We're not wasteful people."

Mike was only half listening. The nut cheese wasn't too bad if
you didn't eat too much of it at once.

. . .

"Won't Liz be angry if we're late?" Inedia asked, licking a bit of
mustard from a corner of her mouth and pushing her glasses back
onto her thin nose.

After a long pause, Ryan said, "What would you say if we didn't
go home, if you and me just"—he looked out the window—"didn't
go home?"

Inedia shrugged. "Could I have warm food?"

"Sometimes." He wasn't sure if she could transition to cooked
food effectively or how this particular meal would sit or if she could
tolerate any cooked food at all. Lisbeth said you needed special en-

zymes or something to go back. If he brought Inedia home with an upset stomach today, Lisbeth would be suspicious. And if she found out about the burger, she might make them do another cleanse.

Where would they go anyway? There was only Lisbeth's mother, temporarily. He could use Inedia as barter, but then what? The last time he saw Eileen, when Inedia was only a month or two old, she'd cried, looking at Lisbeth's and Inedia's respective small frames, and said, "Such a shame, so much wasted." She hovered over the baby carrier, hesitating as though she feared she might break the tiny child.

The pictures of Lisbeth on her parents' mantel in Nebraska looked like they were from a badly written independent film. In each she wore a variation of her Catholic school uniform accented by evidence of her latest fad. In ninth grade, heavy eyeliner, caked-on ghoulish powder, and dark purple lipstick; in tenth, a groover's candy necklace layered over a plastic child's necklace, Barbie earrings, and a thick hemp head scarf. Her twelfth-grade photo showed a Lisbeth closest to her present appearance, the gaunt bones in her face hinting at what Lisbeth called an "intentional experiment with anorexia." There was no eleventh-grade picture; "Lisbeth had decided she could not be photographed," not because it would steal her soul, but "for reasons she couldn't pronounce," her mother had said, walking Ryan through the collection. "Such a shame there's no picture. She had gotten rid of the blue highlights and taken to wearing Victorian gowns around the house."

RYAN PICKED AT the flat hamburger and focused on the fries. What if Lisbeth picked up breatharianism, Inedia's namesake, next? They'd have to give up the fruit-based diet and be sustained solely by their prana and sunlight, no food. His prana hadn't increased on the fruit or with a daughter as it was; all his prana was wasted on grazing and making poop and worrying about Lisbeth and the money.

He knew of Lisbeth's tendencies toward a kind of all-or-nothing fanaticism. Though she would never admit it, Lisbeth had enjoyed Catholic school, despite her stated principles of anarchy and atheism. As her mother put it, "Lizzie would tell you she hated that school, but at public school she would have only blended in; she needed something to rebel against. And anyway, she's always been into rituals. She may not believe in God, but she liked praying at the same time every day; she liked crossing herself. There was no middle ground with her, even as a young girl. One summer she wouldn't step on any cracks; the next, she went out of her way to step on all of them, probably to kill me." Eileen giggled.

There was something about Lisbeth's hatred of her mother that Ryan could never justify. Lisbeth had told her mother about her assault in a fit of anger one day, screamed it as though Eileen were the rapist. "You don't get to cry over my body, Mother," Lisbeth had said. Her mother, as far as she was concerned, had no part in the grief. Ryan couldn't understand how Lisbeth came out so damaged when her parents were, by all appearances, loving and stable. It was as if the more she had, the more reasons she found to criticize it. Lisbeth had never been to therapy, but she toyed with the idea of getting certified to provide "lifestyle support" to like-minded families. There was no way she would accept an intervention, though that might make for a better reality series.

To Inedia, Ryan said, "Let's go over some of your vocabulary words so we can say you did some of your lessons today. What's"— he didn't know why he chose the word—"consumption?"

Inedia tucked a two-inch piece of bread into her mouth and said, without looking up from the empty plate, "to eat, or get eaten."

. . .

"I can talk about my polyamory." Lisbeth's voice sounded high pitched and desperate as the crew packed the equipment. "I can call Ben, my newest lover, and have him come over. He's only eighteen. I mean, he's almost eighteen. Actually, he's still seventeen. He's underage. And he's black. Most of them are black!" she called over to the men moving into the truck. "You guys aren't going to find another polyamorous, detached mother in an interracial family of fruitarians."

"Liz, it's okay," Mike said, blowing smoke over his right shoulder. It was after five, early to end a shoot, but he was tired of stalling. He should give up, start a new career, listen to his mother and settle down with a nice man, but he said, "We'll schedule a day to come back, when everyone's here. I'm just gonna grab the paperwork I need you to sign." He headed toward the van.

A car pulled into the driveway. Ryan, seeing the van and Lisbeth outside, said, "Stay in the car, Inedia."

Lisbeth ran toward him, her performance for Mike uneven. "What do you think you're doing? You could have just cost us everything." She whispered, "The money."

Ryan brushed past her toward the house. He wanted to grab some clothes for Inedia.

"He's here, Mike." The relief showed through Lisbeth's tense smile. "Guys, we can get started again. They're here."

Ryan turned back from the house and walked onto the lawn, carrying a super-size carton of french fries. "Right, I'm here, Mike." He barely raised his voice, looking at no one in particular. Then he bent over as if observing something in the grass. Lisbeth grabbed Ryan's arm, turning him to face Mike, who puffed, silent, sensing something was about to change. The analogy he was searching for to describe Lisbeth, Mike realized, was Little Edie twirling, or maybe Gloria in *They Shoot Horses, Don't They?*

"Guys," Mike yelled toward the open van. "Jonathan, camera, now. Get the boom."

Jonathan had been in the back seat playing a game on his phone, talking loudly to the others about how this pilot was never going to happen. Now he moved too slowly to catch much of it.

Ryan pulled french fries from the red carton, stuffing his mouth with them like a row of long yellow fangs. He threw some of the fries at Lisbeth, took small bites, and threw more.

Lisbeth was scream-crying. "Get that carcinogenic trash out of your mouth, Ryan, now." Inedia's face pressed against the car window, her mouth open and gulping, making circles of condensation.

"It's not fruit, Ryan. What's wrong with you? It's not fruit!" Lisbeth shouted.

BACK IN THE car, Ryan asked Inedia if she was okay.

"Yes," she said, sounding a little breathless, but her face was flush with life.

Ryan would call and check on Lisbeth in a few days, to see if she would accept his conditions for reconciliation, to say he tried, though he already knew the outcome.

MIKE HAD LOST Ryan, but his vision was clear now. With one of Lisbeth's lovers they could reenact this scene; the show would go on, with this Lisbeth or another. The stuff passed right through you, even when you were full or sick, leaving more holes, a hunger. Of course the show would go on.

SUICIDE, WATCH

Jilly took her head out of the oven mainly because it was hot and the gas did not work independently of the pilot light. Stupid new technology. And preferring her head whole and her new auburn sew-in weave unsinged, and having no chloroform in the house, she conceded that she would not go out like a poet.

But she updated her status, just the same:

> *A final peace out*
> *before I end it all.*
> *Treat your life like bread,*
> *no edge too small*
> *to butter.*

Jilly was not a poet or even an aspiring one. She just liked varying her posts as much as possible. She had 1,672 Facebook friends and 997 Twitter followers, and she collected them like so many merit badges. The beautiful mixed friend with the blond curls meant that pretty people liked Jilly, too. And being friends with the mahogany-colored guy with the enviable and on-trend tapered beard with all the followers on Instagram—the one who liked one of her baby pictures a year ago—was almost the same as having a fine black boyfriend when all the research and a popular video said it was a good thing black women already knew how to dance to "Single Ladies" because that was going to be their song forever.

Her friends included her mailman; five of the checkout boys at Stater Brothers on Riverside Avenue, three from Foothill in Fontana, and one from the grocer Ralphs in Rialto; all sixty-four of her mom's friends from high school, many of whom had known her in utero; the podiatrist who removed the bursitis from her left big toe in seventh grade; her therapist from high school; her therapist from undergrad (her current therapist had a no-friending policy); all her high school teachers; the professor with whom she slept and two with whom she didn't; her third-grade best friend; her birth buddy from the hospital, who had been born exactly one minute after her, and who had been particularly difficult to find since her name had changed; as many mutual friends as said yes; and countless people who'd sent her LinkedIn requests, despite her disdain for that particular networking ploy.

Jilly determined to wait at least four hours before checking the status of her farewell post so she wouldn't look desperate, but then she remembered that she didn't have long left, so she waited five minutes and checked her phone.

Four notifications:

JULIA WEINBERG, KAREN GRANT, AND 2 OTHER PEOPLE
RECENTLY LIKED YOUR STATUS.
JESSICA GIVEN [that was Jilly's mom]
COMMENTED ON YOUR STATUS.
REMINDER: YOU HAVE 1 EVENT THIS WEEK.

Six more people had liked her other status, about a juice cleanse she was considering, from earlier in the day.

She didn't know how to interpret the likes on her poem. Was it too cryptic? Were people happy she was saying goodbye, sanctioning her death? Jilly checked the third notification on the list. The Studio Center art show was on Friday, and she had already picked out an outfit. She drew her feet under her hips and sank deeper into the couch. She ignored the text message and two subsequent phone calls from her mother, who must have seen the poem and interpreted it properly. So it wasn't too cryptic. She opened the clock app and set her phone timer to one hour, then got up and put her phone in the microwave, a trick she'd taught herself to keep from checking it obsessively, because the act of having to retrieve the phone was supposed to be such a bother that she'd get tired of doing it.

Since she was already in the kitchen, Jilly removed the pouch from the utility drawer—she liked calling it that, a utility drawer, though many of the things in it (the stubs of crayons too small to use, pennies stuck together, widowed locks and keys) were no longer useful—then removed the box cutter from the pouch. She sat back on the couch, trying to decide on the best place to be found with slit wrists. A bloody mess in the kitchen would make it look unplanned, her life taken abruptly in a fit of desperation. The shower, on full blast while she sat under its stream, would make less mess but look desperately premeditated. The bathtub, where the blood would pool—she couldn't even think of the bathtub. She had seen *Harold and Maude* in a sociology class, and it scared her, all kidding aside. Most blood did, in fact. She put the knife back in its pouch and thought it a shame, because it was a cute knife and pouch, with matching kawaii cupcakes on the handle and flap.

She checked her pages again, this time on her laptop.

Pills might not work the first time. All she had were six pseudoephedrine-free gelcaps, and they seemed most likely to upset her stomach. There was no alcohol in the house to mix with anything, because she drank only when people could watch. She was really funny when she drank, or at least she tried to be. Her impression of Shirley Temple as Heidi was a big hit. "I've got to see the grandfather, I've just got to," she would say, bunching up her lips and hunching her shoulders. She'd tap-danced on a table once or twice to applause.

On the bright side, if the suicide attempt failed and she had to have her stomach pumped, she would lose at least ten pounds, and that would be better than last year's colonic, the pictures of which had elicited an awkward silence from her online friends. Weight loss would make for a great status update.

Razor wounds were better, she decided, because even though there would be blood, she'd pass out before she saw much of it, and if she didn't die, she could take pictures of the scars. Actually, scarring might be much better than attempted or completed suicide because there'd be questions to answer, like "What happened? Who did that to you? Are you okay? Do you need help with anything? You didn't do that to yourself, did you?" She committed to becoming a cutter for an hour or so, like Ellie on *Degrassi*, and to make a few marks up one arm and then post a picture. She eyed her marmalade cat, Sherman, sitting on the window's lily-print cushion. The cuts would have to be deep enough so they wouldn't look like mere scratches but not so deep as to draw too much blood.

The first tiny cut hurt way more than it looked like it did when Ellie tried it, and Jilly was hungry. She put the knife back in its pouch, again, licked at her wrist—though there was no blood, only a superficial abrasion—rifled through the pantry, and finding nothing to snack on, sat back on the couch.

She had read somewhere, a book in Psychology 101 or something, that people who told everyone they were going to do it were just asking for permission, but she didn't need or want permission.

. . .

The thing about Jilly—and this is something she'd feared about her life from adolescence onward—was that there was no backstory. Nothing exciting or terrible had ever happened to her, and if there was any oppression for her to overcome, it only grazed her but never lingered. She had been followed in posh boutiques many times by Asian and white women and twice by black women, but those were the only examples of racism she could remember experiencing. She knew that she should feel discontentment, connected to a large chain of disenfranchisement or systemic persecution— it's not that black death and the news of the world didn't touch her spirit—but she was somewhat ashamed to say, in therapy or publicly, that the bulk of her discontentment came from having very little about which to be discontented. Her mother was pushy but stable, her father claimed her, her friends were attentive if tired. It was she who broke up with her boyfriend, not the other way around, and they were still Facebook friends. She got a dozen "Are you okay?" direct messages after she changed her status from "in a relationship" to "single." And she had a full network of supportive people, however superficial most of their interactions were. The support she lacked felt more fundamental, and she didn't know where to seek it.

The picture Jilly had posted the day before had gotten only four likes and two comments: "HOTT," from an acne-prone creep she'd known in high school; and "your welcome" when she replied to his post. Perhaps that was what set her off, not disregard for the difference between "you're" and "your," but the shallow comments. She thought the picture, which she'd taken in her bathroom mirror from her camera phone, warranted a better response, at very least because of the interesting angle from which she took it. The sideways shot showed her, fingers making a peace sign, lips making a fish face, in a cream-colored skirt that stopped at the upper thigh and offset her smooth brown skin, and a purple bandeau top that might or might not have been half of a bikini.

She put her laptop down and pulled her knees toward herself when an idea came to her. It was Thursday, after all. She posted "TBT" and a link to a YouTube video of "Dead and Gone," to feel out the traffic, then waited for the notifications to start, for the thumbs to erect small monuments.

Within twenty minutes, a red square announced fourteen likes, no comments. She didn't know how to read this. Were they saying they wanted her dead and gone or that they liked TI, or Justin Timberlake?

She waited ten minutes and tried a second video, then another, posting from her laptop. These things worked best in a quick succession that made them seem stream of consciousness. "Another one: 'Give Up the Ghost' by Immature, feat. Crazy Bone."

"Oh and can't forget Bone Thugs: 'Crossroads.'"

Jilly could boast of few superlatives that might be included in her obituary. In eighth grade, she was voted Most Photogenic by her peers and earned a quarter-page feature in the school yearbook. But she could never regain that former glory. By high school, she was one of four Prettiest Girls, and two of them were thicker than she was, and she wasn't even the only black girl to win the honor. An undergrad boyfriend said she was the best kisser he'd ever had, but he cheated on her. A stranger at the mall said her feet were "the most adorable feet I've ever seen." She wasn't sure if the compliments of a creeper even counted. What did she have to show for her life, other than the near perfections of her appearance?

She did actually feel depressed now, thinking about it, dying and all. No one would associate her with Sylvia Plath. She wouldn't look like the Lady of Shalott with her new weave framing her face as she lay on her back in a boat, or even Anne of Green Gables as the Lady of Shalott or even Megan Follows as Anne of Green Gables as the Lady of Shalott, because her natural hair wasn't even red, and anyway, she'd read that when black women died it wasn't glamorous, and people didn't make metonymic literary connections about them, even to lynching— as they did for black men; black women's bodies just died, out of frame, and that made her sadder.

The laptop pinged. Another notification.

"Love this song! You're on a roll today, girl."

· · ·

If Jilly were to run a content analysis of the style and type of posts that got the most responses, it would emerge that faux Ebonics always ranked high, especially up until the past year or so: "Peep this foos." A picture of herself wearing red oversize Sally Jessy Raphael glasses and making a fish face was one of her all-time highs, with 384 likes and 73 comments; maybe yesterday's reenactment photo, in the white skirt and purple bandeau, was just played out. Current events worked, if they were interesting, deep stories she'd seen on Yahoo News about medicines that actually made you sicker or soy milk filled with estrogenic compounds and neurotoxic proteins. Posts about television were even better: "Kerry Washington is SO gorgeous. I want that outfit . . . and that one. Go, Shonda!" Instant fifty-six likes. Cat videos outperformed babies, which followed closely behind, but delicate posts about family and #blessings could be tricky, because people didn't want to see how happy you were too often, even if you were making it all up.

· · ·

Jilly returned to the kitchen and scanned the refrigerator. Several of her friends were on antidepressants and had attempted suicide before, and they got a lot of positive responses for their candor. Jilly had asked her third therapist for antidepressants twice, but she said, "No, Jilly, I'm still not that kind of doctor. And you aren't depressed, just narcissistic, and there are, so far, no medications for that."

In third grade, after reading *The Secret Garden*, Jilly had asked her mom—and subsequently two doctors—for a back brace to treat her scoliosis, like Colin. They had all laughed and said, "What an imagination," in those adult voices.

Her second therapist said, "You're not a hypochondriac; you just have too much time on your hands. Try volunteering somewhere."

The old people in the nursing home looked uninterested when Jilly tried out her tap-dancing and Shirley Temple imitations. A man with long ear-and-nostril hairs fell asleep midact, and his snoring was so obnoxious that Jilly paused the show to try to rouse him.

Jilly thought going to and posting vaguely about therapy at least left something up to the imagination of her followers. She mentioned her experiences there frequently in her "Think About It" Tuesday posts, with captions like, "Who says black people don't go to therapy?" and #therapy. If she mentioned it often enough, without saying why she went, people could fill in a sexier disease than narcissism, which you couldn't exactly tell anyone you had, because it made you look bad, and she didn't even have the malignant kind or the official personality disorder; even her narcissism was pastel pink, kawaii cute.

Jilly was really hungry now, and dying of starvation wasn't a quick suicide option. She had a cabinet full of groceries, some even gourmet, but a meal of microwave ramen seemed more fitting for the occasion than, say, chicken tenders and broccoli. She chose one of the Thai-flavored packages from the cupboard.

She had forgotten to put water in her ramen a year ago and heated the dry noodles and powder sauce to a smoky black mess that left her kitchen smelling like burned fish for a week but which made for an excellent photo. 227 likes.

During senior year, she'd known a girl named Fatima who had bulimia, and though Fatima didn't otherwise eat dairy, she often binged on big servings of nacho cheese. Jilly didn't envy any sickness that made you throw up or poop uncontrollably or look so gaunt that you weren't even pretty anymore, but it did seem that everyone else had a label, that their illnesses got more attention, that there was something chic about them.

One of her friends—not online, but her real friend—Carl from the eleventh-grade art club, at Eisenhower High School, had even died. He hadn't asked anyone for permission or left a note. His mother and friends, even Jilly, had wept openly at his funeral.

Jilly shivered, thinking about Carl in the closed casket, and his mom's eyes, glassy yet hollow. She took out a porcelain bowl, which she'd ordered from Etsy, printed with kawaii lollipops.

She'd heard people, including Carl's sister, say that suicide was the ultimate act of selfishness, that it left everyone else behind to clean up the mess. Jilly wasn't sure how she felt about that. It was Carl's body and therefore his choice. And no matter how you died, it left a mess for someone else to clean up. If Carl had died in a car accident or from cancer, his family would have still asked why, and they would have still been responsible for the funeral arrangements.

Jilly chose a porcelain soup spoon and floral-printed chopsticks and placed them next to the bowl. Who would make the arrangements for her? Her mother didn't even know her favorite flowers, and she would probably want Jilly buried in an Ann Taylor dress suit with a bedazzled collar. The auburn sew-in weave was cute, but Jilly wasn't sure she wanted to be memorialized in it forever. Who would run her online tribute page or make sure the right people came to the service? And what good was a funeral if she couldn't, like Tom and Huck, witness the mourners and see how much they had all loved her?

She chastised herself for her stupidity and chuckled. She was not going to kill herself, certainly not today. Maybe she would try volunteering again, try reading to the elderly. She could wear a costume and visit sick children or attractive young men in the hospital; she could start brainstorming the outfits and completing the necessary applications as soon as she finished her dinner. The pictures she would post. Nothing was more fulfilling, it occurred to her, than giving back to others and letting people know about it.

She poured water from the filter pitcher into the bowl, over the dehydrated noodles and powder, and put the whole deal into the microwave and pressed start before she remembered her phone.

Later, those who mentioned her asked whether anyone had noticed anything different about her. Were there any warning signs? And why did she set the whole house and the poor ginger cat on fire? Why did she use the phone instead of a more traditional way? But in the moment, Jilly saw only the bright crimson of the explosion. It came in four red pops, like notifications, friend requests.

WHISPER TO A SCREAM

The comments poured in steadily, and though she never responded to them right away, sometimes taking up to a week so as not to look too eager, Raina always read them almost as quickly as her viewers posted. She ignored anyone who posted comments with the N-word, monkey references, and black-fetish cracks, their vitriol one of the main reasons for her mother's opposition to Raina's "hobby." But the eighteenth comment, "Can u where ur Dorsey uniform in the next 1?" made her close her laptop for a moment before she could bring herself to reopen it. No avatar accompanied the screen name, Sir_Pix_Alot, but she knew it must be Kevin or one of the other guys in her class again. No matter how many times she blocked them, they always reappeared with new names and the same line of trolling. "We know it's you, Raina." "How come you never talk like that to us at school?"

She closed the laptop again and carried it from her bedroom into the bright kitchen, where her mother had left two notes on the oversize refrigerator: "At the salon. Heat the leftovers around 6:30," and "Finish your algebra 2 before you get on Youtube." Raina crumpled both notes into the trash can and reset the magnets—one advertising her father's car dealerships and one for the family dentist—that had held the notes to the fridge. The scrunched paper made a satisfying sound that her viewers would enjoy. Her mother had hidden or thrown out the tasty bread again. "Fiber will help you with some of that belly," Carmen had said the week before, on her way out to some event, focusing her eyes on Raina's midsection for longer than necessary.

Over her snack of baked corn chips with hummus and dried cranberries, Raina replayed the video. "Hi, everyone," her video self whispered from the kitchen table, as her manicured hands stroked alternately a feather and a children's anthology. "Today, I thought I'd"—she ran her fingernails over the cover of the book—"start with some scratching sounds and then tell you a story." She had carefully edited out the two-second frame in which she cleared her throat, fearing it too jarring a sound, despite the six or so requests she'd gotten for "more rasp." She had briefly considered deleting the three-second accidental shot during which she adjusted her breasts into her top, but she kept it for her mother's sake, and for Dom's, deliberating only as long as it took to hit Finalize. She liked leaving Carmen little surprises here and there, sometimes to keep her on her toes, sometimes to force her hand. Last week it was a pendant necklace that grazed her cleavage. The week before, she decided on the hint of a lacy bra under a V-neck shirt.

She guesstimated that Carmen was responsible for seven of the three-hundred-plus views the video gained in its first hour after publication, because just as her mother could check Raina's browser history—which Raina always cleared, along with her cache—Raina could check stats on her viewers, a detail that Carmen did not seem to understand. Her mother must have watched the video from the salon and was probably preparing her lecture.

Dom hadn't seen it yet or he would have called, though at four thirty it was still a little early.

A year ago, when Raina had started making ASMR videos, she assumed that keeping her head out the frame would preserve her anonymity at some level, prevent the sorts of dramas that had resulted from the makeup and hair videos she started in eighth grade. With only her voice and torso as markers, she believed her classmates would not be able to identify her, but someone always did. It wasn't as though she could start over with a new online identity every time they caught up with her; her viewers wouldn't know how to find her, and if she gave them clues, Kevin or the other guys would find them, too. Why should she lose her growing number of subscribers or the stats on her videos because of a few jerks with too much time on their hands?

"Because it isn't right, the whole thing," her mother had said barely a week earlier. "You don't want people to see you as one of those nasty girls, do you." Carmen had phrased it as more of a statement than a question.

"What's nasty about helping people sleep or soothing them?" Raina had said, regretting it almost immediately. That was the point of trying to create an autonomous sensory meridian response, a tingling of the head and body in full relaxation that some people experienced from sounds and other stimuli. Raina was sure some viewers were using it for grosser purposes—some of the comments made that clear—but she saw her videos, and ASMR, as therapeutic. She imagined her voice like warm water pouring over the crown of her listener's head. A girl with PTSD had written to her last week, saying, "Your stories, your voice, these are the only things that have helped me sleep."

"See, Mom," Raina said, showing Carmen this email.

Her mother adjusted her freshly straightened hair—it was always freshly straightened, because Carmen didn't allow it to become unfresh, kinky, even wilted. "We both know that's not what most of the people are using the videos for. It would be different if you weren't whispering and trying to make your voice like that"—Carmen emphasized the last word—"or if your whole head were in the video."

Raina tuned out the rest of the lecture, which involved one iteration or another of the same: Why don't you reconsider plus-size modeling if you want to be in videos and make money? You could try my agency again. Or at least go back to doing hair-and-makeup tutorials so people can see how pretty your face is, instead of them just watching your chest jiggle while you talk. You said yourself you don't feel safe with those perverts and racist folks on there.

"Safe" was the word that Raina actually heard each time the lecture ended. It bothered her that her mother felt more concern over anonymous perverts or racists typing lewd comments from remote places than she felt for the bully down the block, the one at school. Raina did not feel safe, not with Kevin still tracking her online, not when he lingered near the school lockers. She had never felt completely safe at Dorsey, not since fifth grade, when Kylie S. had said that first through fourth grade, sleepovers, and years of after-school ice-skating lessons didn't matter anymore. She could no longer hang out with the only black girl, because her dad said it was "kind of like the fox and the hound and how they had to go their own ways eventually." Even with her handful of friends, Raina felt exposed at Dorsey, hypervisible, the girl with the big chest, the hefty girl, the black girl, the hefty black girl with the big chest. Kevin didn't help matters, always singling her out.

. .

At a quarter to five, she put on her headset with the 3-D microphone and called Dom.

"Hey, sorry, I was finishing something up," his torso said.

"Hey," Raina said, too loudly before correcting herself. "Hey," she half whispered, half spoke. Dom preferred her onscreen persona—no head—and she tolerated his requests for faceless chatting, though she occasionally got a glimpse of his neck or the faint dark scruff on his pale, almost translucent, chin. "What did you think?"

"Hmm, it was good," Dom said after a hesitation. "The story part was. Rapunzel was a nice choice, but if you're gonna do something like that, I think you should show more of your hair next time."

Raina was trying to transition her hair from relaxed to natural, though she kept it flat-ironed in most of her videos. She tried scrunching the burned-straight ends to blend them with the three to four inches of ingrowing coils and kinks at her hairline. But that made her hair only chin length instead of shoulder length, and Dom speculated that her views decreased when her hair was not in the frame or the thumbnail preview for the video.

They had met—really, started chatting, first through text and then on camera—after he commented on a few of her videos. She only had fifty-seven subscribers then, but with Dom's suggestions, little things, like telling stories on camera or changing the video tags, she had grown her brand to over twenty thousand subscribers in a little over five months, even making some advertising revenue.

"Okay, more hair," Raina whispered. "Anything else?"

"Meh, I like the whole fairy-tale theme. I think more videos like that, especially if you dressed up."

"Like a corset?"

"Yeah, something like that." She thought she heard Dom chewing something.

"I'll think about it," Raina said, her mind already working out the details of her mother's reproof. Costumes were especially offensive to Carmen and more evidence of impropriety or kink, not simply roleplaying or fantasy. In her regular voice, Raina said, "Dom, have you thought about what I said, about the next level?"

Dom shifted in his chair, his white hands fluttering toward the top of the screen and out of the frame, probably running through his hair. He was definitely chewing. "I just think it might change things, like, too much," he said, after a long pause. "I like things the way they are now."

"I do, too," Raina said, slowly, back in her gentle-whisper voice, "but if you're really my boyfriend, it would make more sense to actually see each other, or at least more of each other."

"I'll think about it," he said. "My dad's texting me, gotta go. I'll call or something tonight." Raina didn't hear his phone buzzing, but she said bye.

. . .

Knowing her mother would not be home for another two hours at least, Raina checked the comments.

Earthworm366: Dude, you seriously just gave me a brain orgasm. Didn't now that was possible

168 thumbs up

AnimeAniME: Comment hidden due to low rating. Show Comment: U gave me an actual orgasm

147 thumbs down

RhiRhi#1Fan: RIANWHISPER YOU NEED TO GET ON HERE AND
AND MAKE SOME MORE VIDEOS SO I CAN SLEEP. U HAVE THE
BEST TRIGGERS!! ALL TINGLES ALL THE TIME
37 thumbs up
NiceGirlFinishFirstorSecond: love this. one request: can you make a
roleplaying vid about rolling cigars???
12 thumbs up
Lalalalalaland: Why is it that this video is most popular with men
and boys ages 18–64? SMH. Just saying.
80 thumbs up

She appreciated the positive feedback, but sometimes Raina felt,
briefly, that everyone wanted or saw only a piece of her, not a whole,
that she was mere flesh, a series of keywords to help identify her:

ASMR whispers rain tingles black African American
African-American full thick DDs long-hair-don't-care
natural curly massage soft spoken binaural bob ross water
sounds storytelling hair brushing gentle role play adenoids
spa day fairy tales tapping mind massage autonomous
sensory meridian response breasts cleavage

As she deleted one of the latest offensive comments, which
were fewer and farther between this round, her eyes found another post, clearly from Kevin or one of his sidekicks, maybe
Adam or Michael.

SmexyandIKnowIt: I want it you got it lemme
get it come on wit it Raina.

This one was probably Michael's work; his punctuation was always the worst of the three guys, even though he sat three seats to the left of Raina in AP English now. Kevin was their leader of sorts. He had been nicer in elementary school, though his mean edge was present if you crossed him. Raina almost liked him then, admiring his short brown hair and the way his green eyes contrasted with his tan. But around sixth grade, he became really mean to a lot of the girls, not just Raina, though he often made comments about the size of her chest. It was only when he tried to feel her up on a class trip to Catalina that they became enemies. She had pushed him into a row of kayaks, causing him to knock them over. Crying, she ran off; he told his friends—and subsequently the entire class—that Raina was a slut who had flashed him her boobs.

She hadn't felt safe around him since. Occasionally, he caught her when she was isolated, after school or near her locker. Once, a month ago, he whispered some of the things he would do to her, that first he was going to grab her breasts and then cut one of them off. Raina hadn't told anyone at first. It would be her word against his, just as it had been the time she told her mother and the principal about the incident in Catalina. Her mother had said she wanted to "deal with this situation," but she also asked Raina, "Did you do anything to make him think he could touch you like that? Did you give him any ideas?" Carmen wouldn't understand these whispers any more than she understood why Raina wanted to leave Dorsey. And anyway, Kevin didn't put any actual threats in writing. She had no proof—with his many avatars and handles—that any of the online harassment even came from Kevin or whether Kevin would act on anything he said. But sometimes she wondered if the stress of the ongoing, implied danger might be just as harmful. It was the idea of the idea of Kevin that kept Raina anxious.

She blocked SmexyandIKnowIt before looking at the recent uploads from other ASMR channels. Raina was one of only a handful of black ASMR providers, and so far only one other black girl had more subscribers than she, but that girl was older and had been making videos longer. Raina hoped to compete with the nonblack majority of ASMR makers, some of whom had hundreds of thousands of followers and videos with millions of views. If she counted her previous two YouTube names, she had a total of three million views—though at least a thousand of those were probably from Carmen. Under her current name, Rainwhispers, Raina's most-watched video was at nearly 900,000. Her income from the videos meant she could bypass her father and buy herself the 3-D headset she used with Dom and in her videos, but she didn't make big purchases often.

Her mother never relented in her disapproval of the means, but she approved of Raina's profits and agreed that a money market account would help Raina secure her future, without having to depend on a man, even her father. "All of this, this lifestyle, isn't just from the divorce settlement," Carmen reminded Raina regularly, pointing around the house. "I was on the payroll. Always make sure you're on the payroll." She wondered if her mother knew that it wasn't her father's money that burdened her, but the way her mother showed it—Dorsey, the Town Car, endless luncheons and benefits. Raina vowed to send her own kids to public school, somewhere where they'd never be the only one of anything, and to create as safe and nurturing an environment as she could.

. . .

Carmen blew in through the house around seven, her hands full of large brown-and-white paper bags with twine handles. She filled the room, despite her thin frame. "Did you eat?" she asked Raina, who was seated at the kitchen island, half watching a reality show and half thinking about what Dom said.

"Just finished one chicken breast and the Brussels sprouts you left." Raina sighed. She was still hungry and planning on raiding the freezer for whatever stevia-sweetened sorbet or other low-carb snacks she could find once her mother was out of the room.

"Good. The family commercial is coming up in two weeks, don't forget."

"I know, you've told me three times and left a note."

"I never know if you read them or just throw them away," Carmen said, smoothing one of her brown bags off the counter. "I picked a few things out for you. How was your day, by the way?"

Raina shrugged. She debated telling her mother about Kevin, again, but instead said, "Fine. We had a sub in English today, so I got my homework done during class. The video is doing pretty well so far."

"Hmm," Carmen said, her lips pinched together as she rifled through the shopping bags. "I wish you had left out the boob shot, but the story was cute. I'm thinking this blue one is the best dress for the commercial; your father will be in blue, though I'll probably wear gray or green—I haven't decided."

"It looks too small," Raina said, getting up to feel the fabric of a navy blue A-line dress with a narrow rhinestone belt attached to the waist. "It's a 10/12," she said louder than she had planned, though she could never control her voice with Carmen. "I'm a fourteen. You know that."

"Yes, but you have two weeks," Carmen said, smiling a little and pointing to another bag. "They're all twelves. At least look at them. I spent an hour of my day looking for pieces that would be flattering."

"I'm supposed to be calling Dom soon," Raina said, and left for her bedroom.

. . .

Raina sat on her bed, turned on her television, and considered using her trump card—"I can go stay with Dad, then"—but this battle didn't seem worth it, at least not yet. Maybe if Carmen pushed again about Raina getting the edges of her hair touched up, Raina might invoke the idle but still-useful threat. Her dad didn't exactly approve of the videos either, but he said they weren't harming anything as long as she kept them clean. She wasn't sure if he had seen many of them, but when she opened the money market account, he joked, via text message, that Raina was a budding young businesswoman after his own heart and that maybe he'd let her write and direct one of his commercials eventually. He never followed through, even after Raina presented him with a script. "That's so cute, honey," he had emailed. "But we have a professional guy who does that. Love you. Listen to your mother ;)" She emailed him less frequently after that.

Raina hated posing for the commercials. She hunched awkward and chubby against her mother's tall thinness and blended into her father's roundness, their features melding together while Carmen's jutted, smug or confident. Raina inherited her father's bug eyes. "Sad she takes after him," she'd overheard a tipsy aunt say once at a holiday party.

The biannual commercials for her father's car dealerships stopped being cool after about first grade, when she transferred to Dorsey, where the kids of CEOs were not impressed. She tried to laugh it off when Kylie S. and even Megan and Liz, her two friends, joked about the silly slogan her father insisted on. In homage to a DMX song fluffed and smoothed out into R&B, her father sang, "What's our name? Tyson Family Motors. If you want it, we got it, our cars are with it. Come on." The original song came out several years before Raina was born, when they still lived in the foothills of Rancho Cucamonga, and her father, fresh out of undergrad, had inherited and rebranded his parents' dealership, turning one location into four and beginning her family's ascent—really their move west—from one house in the Inland Empire to one in Westwood and a vacation condo in Aspen. They didn't ski; it was pure status symbol, that house. Her father lived in Woodland Hills, about thirty minutes away from Raina, with his girlfriend, Manda, a blond twentysomething who basically treated Raina the same way Carmen did; only she thought Raina's hair "looked so cute that way, with all those little curls." Raina saw them about six times a year, plus the two commercial shoots, which her mother still participated in four years after the divorce, because she and Raina's father both agreed that "the family brand is different from the family."

Scenes from the family brand: Manda standing with a plastered smile, off to the side, off camera; a montage of Raina, Carmen, and Carl Tyson huddled together at the intersection of each dealership and each of her father's billboards; a family existent only in cuts; her dad making promises in a voice-over; the theme song playing over their poses.

. . .

Dom didn't answer when she tried to call him for a video chat, but he texted five minutes later that he would call in an hour.

"How do you know this Dom guy is even a real person?" her friends had asked, sounding exactly like Carmen, for a change. "Haven't you seen *Catfish*?"

Raina knew Dom was real and close to her age, though once he had said seventeen and once he had said fifteen. They had never hung out in person—Dom lived in Connecticut—but she had seen his whole face early on in live video chats, when they used to talk like normal people. It was only after her popularity increased that he started asking her to make it "more like an ASMR video," quiet and without her face. She would wait another day or so before she asked him again about chatting the old way. Anyway, he was supposed come out to California for a summer program, only five months away, he said; at very worst, they'd see each other then.

Carmen knocked on her door and opened it without Raina's consent. "I'm sorry about the twelves, Rain. How about we take you to my Pilates class tomorrow, so you'll feel more confident, lengthen out a little? We can go shopping at the end of the week and you can pick something you like, fourteen, twelve, whatever."

Raina sighed. "I don't want to go shopping, Mom."

"You have to wear something," Carmen started. She sat on Raina's bed. Up close, Carmen's skin was smooth and poreless, nearly as young as Raina's but for a few skin tags. "What is it, Rain?" she said, her voice nearly affectionate, her hand hovering as though it might touch her daughter's shoulder. "You never talk to me anymore."

Raina's mind browsed the possible answers to this tone-deaf statement: That's because you're never home; you don't listen anyway; maybe because everything you say is a lecture; maybe because you care more about how I look than how I feel; I think Kevin's posting anonymously on my page, sexually harassing me, again, and what will you even do about it?

"We can go shopping, but I'm not going to Pilates. Can you leave? I need to call Dom," she lied.

Carmen left with a small huff, mumbling under her breath about teenage moodiness and ingratitude and what would have happened to her if she had used Raina's tone of voice with her mother.

Raina scrolled through her new comments, another one from Kevin. There were still forty-five minutes left before Dom was supposed to call, forty-five minutes to compose herself and fix her voice into something pleasant, order the details of her life so that only the prettiest parts showed.

On days like this, Raina sometimes fantasized about running away, saving her money, taking her equipment, and finding a community of people who would really see her, not the family brand, not the extra thirty pounds, not the untouched edges of her hair or her Web tags, but her, whoever she was, her whole head and body fitting into a frame of her own design. But she knew this community didn't likely exist, and Carmen said that runaways only ended up with human traffickers. She could tolerate Carmen and Dorsey for a few more years until college, couldn't she? But what then? She wanted to think of college as an opportunity for new freedoms, self-expression, rebellion. She would grow her hair out into naps if she pleased and do what she wanted with her body. But what if college was only thirteenth grade, an escalation of everything in her life now, with older, more taxing versions of the same people, where she'd exchange Carmen and Kevin for new avatars—a controlling sorority sister or an inappropriate professor?

RAINA STARTED OUTLINING a new video. She usually wrote a script and storyboard first and improvised her monologue once she began filming, sometimes taking three days for a single concept. She sat in front of the camera, with her 3-D microphone nearby, but she quickly abandoned her notes. With her whole head in the frame, she spoke in her natural voice, softened so that Carmen would not hear her. "Today, I'm not going to tell you a fairy tale, but something I've been thinking about, about myself," she began. "I struggle with a lot of things," she said. "Sometimes, I think I'm beautiful and smart, but then one little thing knocks me down, and I don't know who I am. I can't be the only one who feels this way." She paused. She might have been crying; her voice, sharp and cracking, would not modulate. "I'm tired of faking this whispery voice and doing everything for everyone else and worrying about how I look and if anyone's going to intimidate or abuse me and telling other people's fantasy stories. I want to stop being afraid to tell the truth. I want to say, 'Screw everyone who thinks they can just treat me any kind of way, even my mom and boyfriend.' But would you even hear me?" She persisted until she felt spent, emptied as though after a deep purge. Her exhilaration at the thought of publishing this video made Raina feel slightly breathless. Her cursor hovered over the Upload button.

The laptop rang—Dom calling for a video chat—just as Carmen knocked and barged into the room again. "Raina, what is it? You've been crying. I could hear you from my room. Talk to me, honey. What is it?"

Raina didn't look up at Carmen or pause to decline Dom's call. With the laptop still ringing and Carmen still talking, she canceled the upload and deleted the footage. She could start over later, returning to her fairy tales. Editing was the easiest part anyway; she worked best in short frames, quiet slivers, fragments. Everyone said so.

NOT TODAY, MARJORIE

Marjorie was already frazzled when she entered the DMV. She had tried to stick to her acronym all morning:

> Watch your feelings for a moment
> Acknowledge them
> Imagine your options
> Thoughtfully proceed

Though she had succeeded in avoiding any unseemly confrontations for the past four consecutive days, the ride to the DMV was taxing, the night before tormenting, and she felt her limits approaching. It was one of those afternoons on which, despite her best efforts, she could not see the good, could not practice the options for avoiding conflict that her therapist was making her study, could not replace the word "and" with the word "but," as she had been instructed to do. On a good day, Marjorie was supposed to say, "I'm angry, *and* I can still keep my temper in check," instead of, "I lost my temper, but I couldn't help it." Instead of "I hate crowds, but I have to go to the DMV," on a good day, Marjorie could say, "I hate crowds, *and* I'm still going to keep my wits about me at the DMV."

Today, however, was not a good day. Today Marjorie paused at an Ice Cube song on the radio and felt a shiver of longing for her old lifestyle and her ex-boyfriend Charles. Once she stepped out of her car, she immediately regretted her choice of a black long-sleeved shirt—she always wore long-sleeved shirts—the sun burning straight through the fabric onto her arms. Today Marjorie saw the yellow jackets and the wasps but not the fragrant lavender bushes that lined the front entrance of the DMV. She smelled the icky pollen but did not notice the vibrancy of the goldenrods in the planters. One side of her hair wouldn't lie flat, and though she had spent hours flat-ironing it, the ends of her hair now looked limp, yet the edges looked beady. Today was all buts.

Inside the DMV, grimy children ran around or played with cell phones, families spoke languages Marjorie didn't recognize, squat pregnant women slouched in chairs, their laundry detergent and deodorant pungent. The air conditioner blasted through the space, quickly replacing the heat outside with its own cold oppression. Marjorie had made up her mind to get in and get out with her attitude intact, but already, so many things portended difficulty. You are already stressed *and* you are not going to get worked up, she told herself. Not today, Marjorie.

Marjorie's preferred DMV on Baseline, if one can prefer a DMV rather than simply dread it, was closed for renovation. She scolded herself for waiting until the last minute to renew her license. She scolded herself for taking the advice of her friend Jessica, her only remaining friend, who warned Marjorie to "at least try to renew your license online or go to the Foothill location, since you know you how irritable you can get around crowds. It's nicer at that one, newer building."

Jessica was wrong on three fronts. First, Marjorie could not complete her driver's license renewal online or by phone or by mail because she had mailed in her previous two renewals, so she must appear in person for this one, subjecting herself to new fingerprints, vision tests, and the long lines. Anyway, she would never apply for renewal online because she didn't trust the online system not to steal her identity. That had happened to Coryn White's son Londyn when he renewed his vehicle registration a few months ago.

Second, Marjorie could be perfectly fine in crowds. She attended a church with over ten thousand members, and she had just organized and volunteered at its back-to-school backpack drive three days before, passing out school supplies and nonperishable food items to nearly two hundred families. She had collected many of the supplies herself, shopping the packed stores for inexpensive bulk erasers and glue sticks. It wasn't the crowd at the DMV she dreaded so much as the inefficacy of the place and the many variables that could make the experience ugly. There was so much ugliness in the world now, not least of which included the ugliness of this DMV, dark with cement floors and red walls. And that—the alleged niceness of the DMV—was the third thing about which Jessica was wrong.

Marjorie settled into her chair facing the entrance, avoiding a black blotch that might have been old gum, and adjusted the sleeves of her shirt. She tried to assure herself that it really didn't matter which DMV she chose, because in some ways they were all the same. She would have had to wait in long lines in Fontana and

San Bernardino, and while at one she might have traded filthy up-holstery for these hard plastic chairs, the chairs would be equally uncomfortable no matter the location. And these same kinds of people might have very well been at any DMV. She focused on her breathing, counting to three on the inhalation and five on the exhalation. But this was interrupted by the intrusive staring of a little boy who might have been Latino; she couldn't tell. There were so many immigrants now.

The boy wore a lightweight blue hoodie with the hood pulled so tightly over his face that it squished it into exaggeration. His sneakers were scuffed at the tips, and his eyes carried the insipid-ness of someone who could not entertain himself without televi-sion. Marjorie averted her eyes; she should have brought a book to read. The boy stared. Marjorie grimaced and stuck out her tongue at him. His eyes widened but still had no sheen, and he turned back to his mother, tugging at her sleeve, but she was engrossed in a driving manual and would not look up at him. Served him right, she thought, though she could already feel a little guilt pressing her insides together.

Marjorie didn't have any children of her own, nor did she want any. Her volunteer work stifled any latent biological clock, si-lenced it outright. The children who came to collect the backpacks and school supplies from the church were like wild animals, even the good ones. They were receiving gifts, curated by caring hands, and yet some of them had the nerve to complain, "I don't want a red one." "I want a different backpack, not that one." Marjorie had smiled graciously and fought back her urges to say, "Beggars can't be choosers, now, can they?"

"You should see how some of the mothers dressed them," she had told Jessica after the backpack drive. "Completely inappropriate outfits. One little girl had on a spaghetti-strapped top and shorts and ankle boots with a little heel. I'm talking about a seven-year-old with a little heel."

"The top doesn't sound that inappropriate," Jessica said. "It is summer. Not everyone keeps their arms covered like you."

Jessica knew good and well why Marjorie kept her arms covered—something Marjorie hadn't even told her own therapist, Alex, about yet—so that was a low blow. For a counselor, Jessica could sometimes be insensitive. Not today, Jessica, Marjorie thought.

"And the way they talk," Marjorie had continued. "Some of them sound straight-up illiterate. Don't get me wrong, we had our slang growing up, our Ebonics and what have you, but all this 'I be wanting this,' and 'she be needing that.' The educational system and these parents are failing our black children."

The phone line went silent, and Marjorie was just about to ask Jessica if she was still there when Jessica said, "Yes, you've said that before. How is the therapy going for you?"

Marjorie sniffed, drawing out the sound, and said, "It's going. Not sure how long I'll stick with it. And I thought you weren't going to ask me questions about it, confidentiality and all."

Jessica made some excuse to get off the phone shortly after that.

Jessica attended Marjorie's church, and they had become fast friends about seven months earlier when Jessica joined one of Marjorie's volunteer committees. But she was starting to pull away from Marjorie like a lot of people had recently. Marjorie noticed but did not let on how much this distance concerned her. Pastor Bevis said two Sundays ago, "Sometimes when God lets people leave your circle, it's because they weren't meant to be there. If He shrinks your crowd, it's because not everybody can go where He's taking you." Marjorie had said a very loud "amen" to that and looked at Coryn White, who had formerly been in Marjorie's circle but who must not be going where God was taking her now. Coryn couldn't even compliment her on the success of the backpack drive, she was so bitter. She smiled weakly and wouldn't make eye contact with Marjorie the whole day.

After the phone conversation with Jessica, Marjorie had made a mental note to be more positive. If Jessica stopped talking to her, too, Marjorie would really look like she had no one, and Coryn would win all over again.

The little boy in the hoodie kept glancing at Marjorie cautiously, but he wasn't staring anymore. Marjorie heard that Pastor Bevis was going to use footage of the backpack drive in the announcements that played over the jumbo screens in the church this coming Sunday and personally congratulate her for her hard work. Then Coryn would really have something to feel bitter about. Marjorie giggled a little in anticipation of Coryn's face, then feeling self-conscious, she almost stopped herself. But she remembered, in keeping with her new therapist's advice, she was supposed to feel her feelings, not suppress them, and she kept laughing, right in the DMV.

LIKE THE DMV on Foothill, the therapy was Jessica's idea, and Marjorie had started it, reluctantly, only a month ago with one of Jessica's colleagues, a therapist named Alexandria, Alex for short.

"It might help with some of your trauma—and this whole ongoing issue with Coryn, and your volatility," Jessica had said over the phone; they rarely met for dinner anymore. "Not that I'm judging you—it's just that you have some areas you might want to work on now, while you can. And it's all confidential. I certainly wouldn't talk to your therapist about you."

It was true that Marjorie had been reprimanded a few times at her current job and had left her previous one after a blowup with her manager. In addition to Jessica, more than a few former friends had called her volatile. She was tired of that word. She was not a beaker full of combustible chemicals or a volcano looking for an opportunity to expel pent-up heat, leaving ash and damage in her wake. She was a person, just as much as they were, perhaps more complicated, but certainly normal, just as normal as they were.

Marjorie described herself this way to Alex, during their first meeting and on the intake sheet: "pretty normal, generous with a bit of a temper."

Alex, a petite, brown-skinned black woman, wore her hair pulled tightly in a bun at the top of her head, her glasses olive green and square. She scribbled notes on a pad that she kept next to her on the smaller of two couches, and she never broke eye contact with Marjorie while she wrote.

"That's what I want to work on, the temper, and people say I'm very negative and that I only see the worst." Marjorie was specific in stating her goal, her short-term focus; she did not need to dig up her past or heal from trauma to improve her current behavior, as Jessica had so boldly suggested. She did not want to be one of those people who went to therapy for the rest of their lives, blathering on about what "my therapist said" or "what we uncovered in therapy." It struck Marjorie that those people never got any better; they just used longer and more complicated phrases to say things. Marjorie was tired and spread too thin— that was all—at work, with her volunteering and church duties, with the many dramas of her social life, Coryn. She said as much to Alex, who smiled an ambiguous healthcare professional smile and wrote something down.

"Do you have any examples of what you mean by your temper or your negativity?" Alex asked. When she was not writing, she rubbed her fingers together briskly, in the manner of someone hungry.

Marjorie omitted a few recent incidents with her neighbors and the recent blowup with Coryn and chose her example carefully.

"Last week," Marjorie said, after a pause, "I flung an entire tub of yogurt across my living room. It was raspberry flavored, and the little seeds still had some pulp on them and left marks all over the wall, and every time I see the traces of the stain, I feel mad at myself all over again." She fiddled with the sleeves of her shirt and adjusted each so that it covered her wrists.

"What made you want to throw the yogurt?" Alex asked.

"A lot of things," Marjorie started. Some of the things she didn't want to tell Alex. "I'd had a bad day at work, then I ran into my foster sister Coryn at Ralphs, my grocery store—I don't want to talk about her, but we go to the same church—and then Ralphs didn't have any more of the kind of pickles I like, and when I got home, the yogurt was raspberry instead of strawberry, and somehow I'd picked the wrong kind." Marjorie felt slightly embarrassed, anticipating a scolding. "It wasn't very sanctified of me," she said.

Alex's face didn't show any judgment, but she scribbled on her notepad before she said, "It sounds like it was a hard day. Sometimes it feels good to throw something, maybe not so fun to clean it up."

Marjorie nodded. "There's still this slight yogurt smell in the carpet."

"It seems like the anger didn't just come out of nowhere but had been bubbling for a while. What happened at work before that?"

"I got mad at a customer," Marjorie hesitated. She did not say that earlier in the day she had scrolled through pictures of herself with Charles and felt a suffocating sadness or that when such feelings came up, she often punished herself by pinching at her own arms and legs, digging her nails into old scar tissue until it hurt again. "I'm an account clerk in the bursar's office at a university. I didn't say it loud, but I whispered, 'Go to hell,' just as my manager was walking by, and I already have two strikes, spread out over six months. He gave me a warning look but no incident report. It wasn't nice to say, not a good witness to my church either."

Alex scribbled again. "Had the customer done something wrong?"

"They've always done something wrong." Marjorie could feel her blood pressure rising. "I don't just get mad for no reason. This girl had come in there, and first of all, I saw her cut in line to take a pen from one of the other tellers, and then she was still filling out her slip when she walked up to my counter, and she had made a mistake on her form and tried to argue with me about it. I tried the de-escalation techniques we're supposed to follow, but those kind of customers take a toll on your day."

Alex nodded and wrote; she must have used some kind of shorthand. "It seems like you feel a lot of guilt about your anger. Do you think you might also feel any anger about your guilt?" Alex said, and the subtle profundity of this chiasmus annoyed Marjorie. It was precisely the kind of psychobabble she wanted to avoid and that she sometimes pointed out in Jessica, who would sigh and apologize.

"The Bible says, 'Be angry, and do not sin,'" Marjorie said, ready to pack her purse and go, "so if I have guilt, it's over what I said, which was a sin, not over being angry."

"Listen to that statement," Alex said. "You're allowed to *be* angry and still not sin. Do you give yourself a chance to feel the anger?"

"What do you mean, 'feel the anger'? I told you I threw a tub of yogurt and whispered 'Go to hell.'" Marjorie was beginning to think Alex was a little slow.

"But did you try to suppress those negative feelings, or did you pause to accept that you were angry?" Alex said. Her fingers moved rapidly; there was something squirrelly about her. Marjorie made up her mind that she wasn't coming back. But Alex stood and, after fiddling in her desk, handed Marjorie a worksheet and sat back down on the couch.

"I'd like to work with you if you want to keep coming," she said. "Do you know what a dialectic is? That two or more things can be true at once? So you can feel how you feel—and you can observe that emotional side of your mind and really feel it—and you can still make a choice not to follow it." She pointed to her head, fingers still moving. "We can recognize our emotions without either negating them or letting them dictate our response, as in 'I feel like I could eat every cookie in sight, but I know I shouldn't.' Instead of invalidating your feelings, you would say, 'I want to eat everything in sight, *and* I'm still going to have only one chocolate chip cookie and really take my time eating it.'" Alex leaned back and stopped moving her hands at this.

"So I would say, 'I hate my job and many of the customers who come in—even though as a Christian I'm not supposed to hate—but I'm still going to have a good attitude,'" Marjorie said.

"'And,' not 'but' or 'though,' or 'yet,' which are fake 'buts,'" Alex said. "You'd say, 'I feel some hatred toward some of the customers at my job, and I'm a Christian, *and* I'm still going to have a good attitude.'"

Marjorie didn't see how these subtle semantic shifts would make any difference, in her behavior or her feelings. She could already picture herself becoming one of those people who always talked about what their therapists said, or at least becoming a person who made fun of what her therapist said. But—*and*—she committed to completing the homework assignment over the next week.

THEY WERE TAKING forever to call her number, another reason to regret this DMV. At the one on Baseline, she bet, you could simply stand in line with your check already made out and get your license much more quickly. Here, you had to grab a number and wait. Take a letter and wait. Fill out paperwork and wait. Get fingerprinted and wait. Have your picture—which always comes out looking deranged—taken and wait for the little machine to print out a new license. The entire setup at this DMV was inefficient—even with the new technology and all the blue monitors—routing people through various lines as though they were at Disneyland, where the lines only appeared to shrink because of the ways they wrapped around the dividers. When she was thirty-three Marjorie had won a lawsuit against Disneyland. While there with her boyfriend Charles Stampton, she had slipped in a puddle near Splash Mountain and sprained her ankle. She'd won similar lawsuits from a Denny's restaurant and a ninety-nine cent store in San Bernardino. If these businesses were more efficient, she wouldn't have needed to sue. If Marjorie were running this DMV, there would be two sections with three lines each, one for driving tests and one for plates and registrations and renewals. One could deposit the paperwork and get fingerprinted, have one's vision tested, and take the photograph in a single interaction with a single teller, no numbers, no letters, no sitting, queuing, sitting, lining up again, and waiting over and over.

Marjorie and Alex had discussed this very scenario earlier in the week, to prepare Marjorie to handle her stress in places where she was likely to lose—and historically had lost—her temper. These lines are long and the setup stupid, Marjorie thought, and I am still going to sit here and hold my peace. I have already been mean to a little kid, and I can't change that.

HER FIRST FOUR weeks of therapy were much more cut and dry than Marjorie expected. She had yet to cry or break down, and though Alex seemed relaxed, she gave Marjorie new homework to practice in between each appointment. The replacement of "but" with "and" had started to help, Marjorie could admit after the first week, as had the introduction of an acronym, WAIT, in the second.

"THE POINT IS that we want to calm you down with the pause, so you feel the anger and then proceed wisely," Alex said.

MARJORIE TRIED WAIT at the grocery store and felt a little like a robot, acting from a program instead of her emotions, but she didn't cuss anyone out, even under her breath. Alex's worksheets were not altogether unlike the scripts Marjorie used at work to de-escalate conflict with angry customers, and there was something comforting in the canned process, the shortcuts.

Yet—and—in anticipation of the weekly appointments, Marjorie found herself thinking about what she did not want to say to her therapist, rehearsing safe topics to replace the troubling memories that had begun to resurface, thoughts of Mother Lydia and Coryn, and of the many scars on her arms and their corresponding internal wounds. Marjorie did not want Alex—nonjudgmental or not—to know that some of her volatility was because so many people did not like or respect her and that some of her volunteer work was perhaps penance for sins she had committed. She did not want Alex to know that her drama with her foster sister Coryn resulted partly from Coryn's lingering anger about something Marjorie did. She did not want Alex to know that she had slept with Coryn's husband, Charles Stampton, for years after he married Coryn, and that sometimes, even this morning on the way to the DMV, Marjorie still, albeit briefly, missed him.

MARJORIE'S BLOOD SUGAR was running low and her adrenaline high in anticipation of the continued wait. She yawned in her chair, cold from the overcompensating air conditioner, mildly angry at the discomfort. The AC's assault on her body temperature irritated her. She fished around inside her purse for a peppermint or butterscotch candy and found none. Everything was setting out to steal her joy. "Not today, Satan," she whispered. She hadn't slept well as it was; that was part of the problem. The neighbors, as usual, had hosted a loud party, to which they failed to invite her—perhaps out of racism, perhaps sexism, perhaps out of some anti-Christian sentiment, or perhaps because of Marjorie's yelling match with them seven weeks ago about another party—and she spent the night tossing in bed, listening to the percussive bass line of their music, trying to guess what song it was. It all sounded like New Order or possibly Depeche Mode, but it could have been something new that she'd never heard, since she'd stopped listening to secular music in 1999, except for when she was with Charles.

There were so many people trying to do music now, music that you could barely understand, let alone tolerate. Sometimes the students at the university played their music so loudly you could hear it through their headphones. Marjorie was known for calling right out from her counter in the bursar's office, "Any music that I can hear from your personal device will prevent you from moving through this line." The ones who could hear her would turn it right down, and the ones who couldn't hear her initial threat heard her once she got on the PA system.

Just this morning on Marjorie's way to the DMV, a black twentysomething drove up next to her in a tiny Honda Civic, blaring loud rap music in the new whiny style with his windows down. Even in the unbearable August heat, Marjorie kept her car windows rolled partially down to cut through the condensation of the air conditioner, which made the car too cold. Marjorie was forced to roll her own windows back up because of the invasive music, and she did so with a glare at the young man, who laughed and bobbed his head as the bass still blared but more faintly. It all reminded her of a sounding brass, clanging cymbals. Later in the ride, two other cars cut her off, preventing her from switching into the left lane for an important turn. A stop sign reminded her of her acronym, WAIT, but she was already fuming by then and had to repent for her aggressive use of both middle fingers.

Marjorie was only thirty-seven, but she felt older than her peers; some of them would say she felt better than them, too. But that wasn't true. If anything, she felt inferior for all the many ways she failed at keeping herself unspotted from the world. Marjorie had said the sinner's prayer at age four and rededicated her life to Christ again and again along the way: at fourteen, when she took up smoking; at seventeen, when she lost her virginity; at twenty-two, after a four-year "wild" bender at college; and at thirty-five, when she repented for her six-year affair with Charles Stampton. And she repented regularly for some of her ongoing thoughts, for the times when alone in her bed she still thought of Charles and wanted to touch the places that he used to.

"Do your friends know how hard you are on yourself or how much you care about what other people think?" Alex had asked just last week during their session. "Because it seems like your Christianity offers you grace, but you don't seem to ever offer any to yourself."

Marjorie almost told her about Coryn and Charles then, but she decided against it. Instead she said quietly, "I'm just trying to keep my hands clean, day by day. I've done a lot of bad things in my life, and I've asked for forgiveness, but I feel like I can't stop doing them."

"*And,*" Alex said, "*and* you feel like you can't stop doing them."

ONE DMV TELLER's line moved particularly slowly, and judging from the paperwork in the hands of the people queuing there,

Marjorie guessed it was one of the license renewal lines. She could barely see the teller because she was so short, but Marjorie could see that once people got to her, they appeared to be making a lot of unnecessary small talk. She hoped she wouldn't get stuck with that teller. Marjorie shook her head. She did occasionally make small talk with the students who came to the bursar's office, but nothing that would hold everyone up like this.

The boy in the hoodie and his mother were called into a line, and remembering her grimace, Marjorie felt a little bad. She tried to smile at him, but he frowned and tucked his face into his mother's arm. People could be so unforgiving. It would serve Coryn well to forgive, just as Marjorie had when Coryn tried to have her excommunicated from the church. Such petty nonsense. The Church of God in Christ didn't even practice excommunication. Coryn was remarried now anyway, and without Marjorie's interventions, she never would have known that Charles was a cheater. It was not as though Coryn were blameless herself.

Coryn, Marjorie, and Marjorie's half-sister Latrice had grown up together as foster sisters under the care of Mother Lydia, a fine church lady from all external appearances but an uneven guardian. Mother Lydia made sure all three girls and her two foster sons were well dressed and fed—though in exchange they had to help with the sewing and cooking and grocery shopping. Her temper was frightening. Coryn, light-skinned and two years younger than Marjorie, with hair that was almost honey brown, was Mother Lydia's favorite, Latrice her alternate, Marjorie her scapegoat. Once, Coryn had stolen twelve dollars from Mother Lydia's purse and smiled innocently as Marjorie took the fall. Coryn had sneaked out of the house multiple times during their teen years, and Marjorie got the flack.

"You gotta watch out for your sisters, girl," Mother Lydia had said, "because who do you even have besides me and them? Don't nobody else want you."

Marjorie still bore the scars of Mother Lydia's cigarette burns up and down her arms and on the backs of her legs.

Mother Lydia would sometimes say to Marjorie, pulling her face close to hers, "You remind me of somebody I don't like, and I can't figure out who it is." She never burned her after such speeches, the words searing enough. Marjorie would retreat to the bathroom to examine her round eyes and round face, her small breasts, the marks on her arms, but she could never figure out what Mother Lydia despised in her appearance. On Sundays Mother Lydia was all, "Praise the Lord," and "I'm blessed." Someone in the church must have suspected something was wrong in that house, but if they did, they never let on, and Marjorie was sure—from patchy memories—that whatever Mother Lydia rescued her from was worse than what she gave her.

Certainly Marjorie had forgiven Mother Lydia and Coryn for these wounds, even Latrice, who married young and moved three counties away. Latrice, still married and a teacher now, hadn't spoken to Marjorie since the scandal with Coryn and Charles. Marjorie could have easily brought up the lingering rumors about Coryn, about her son Londyn's questionable paternity and the "spiritual retreat" where Coryn had "assisted" Pastor Bevis while First Lady Bevis was caring for her mother in Oakland. But she didn't. And while Marjorie knew Charles was married to Coryn when she became involved with him, she didn't date him out of any vengeful spirit toward Coryn, she was sure, at first. But when Charles whispered—his stubble against her ear—that he loved

Marjorie's personality, her hips, and the way she moved them, Marjorie couldn't help but feel victorious. She hadn't set out to hurt Coryn; Charles simply liked her better—she fulfilled his needs—just as Mother Lydia had seen something in Coryn that she preferred. These things happened sometimes.

Anyway, Coryn won. She was happily remarried to a man who had legally adopted her son Londyn. Marjorie had only her work, both voluntary and paid—and the anticipated veneration for that work—and occasionally Jessica to keep her busy. Charles fled town after the scandal, after Coryn filed for divorce. Marjorie sometimes feared, especially now that her values were back intact, that she would never find love beyond the Lord.

It might be good for her to talk some of this over with Alex, at least the Mother Lydia parts. Though the burn marks that covered her arms had long healed, sometimes the scars still hurt, and because of Marjorie's self-flagellation they seemed to be living, growing things that reinflamed all the time. Marjorie didn't want to see the marks or give anyone the opportunity to ask about them, so she kept them covered. But as Alex said about concealing feelings, the long sleeves didn't take the pain away.

DESPITE HER SLEEVES, Marjorie wished she had brought a sweater into the DMV. She was freezing, and according to the monitors mounted on the wall, she still had a while to wait.

"Freaking incompetent," a man grumbled as he passed her on his way out of the building. "All this time, and now you tell me I have the wrong form." He yelled back to the tellers, "Thanks for nothing," and stormed out of the building. The space momentarily went silent before it filled with small gasps of pleasure and incredulity at the man's speech. Marjorie had read a study somewhere about why DMVs and banks and similar spaces were known for horrible customer service. It concluded that where the job is low in status but high in power, the customer service will suffer the most. The more discontented the workers, the more discontented the customers. She'd read another story about a man who came to the DMV to pay a $3,000 bill, and in the ultimate act of passive aggression, did so with 300,000 unrolled pennies, distributed in five wheelbarrows carted in with the help of his friends. These kinds of things were the reason why people went postal, employees and customers alike.

Marjorie could understand this in part. The students who came into the bursar's office were often furious before they even got in her line, panicked that their financial aid had not been processed properly or irritated at what they perceived as discrepancies on their accounts. Marjorie's training had taught her how to defuse these conflicts: (1) listen (avoid the word "but"); (2) acknowledge the problem ("Yes, that must be tough"); (3) provide assurance ("I understand, and I can help you"); and (4) even apologize for things that weren't her fault if it calmed the situation.

With some of the ruder students, however, Marjorie practiced what she called retributive finance, smiling her way through their transactions, following the four-step process for de-escalation, and then making certain errors after the students left, to pay them back for bad attitudes or terse conversation. She instinctively felt both guilty and justified for doing this. Her supervisor questioned her once about one of these "errors," and from then on Marjorie staggered her payback just enough to continue undetected. But she felt worse, over time, for making these vindictive adjustments rather than waiting on divine retribution. Her conscience was quicker now to ping her with a twinge of guilt than ever before. Marjorie, for instance, would never hook up with Charles or any married man now. She took this and all the twinges as signs of her continued sanctification, because as Pastor Bevis said, "You get saved once, and that's forever, but sanctification—becoming holy, living right day by day—that's a process, and we're all in that process." Marjorie's process for getting over Charles involved a lot of prayer and digging her nails into her own arms.

The monitor announced Marjorie's turn to approach the fingerprinting line, and she stood up. There were fourteen people ahead of her now, and it was just her burden to be called into the line of the lady who was making small talk with each customer, holding everyone up. Yes, Marjorie could understand why people went postal. She didn't condone it, but she could understand the man's fit as he stormed out of the DMV, could understand the desire to bring pennies, even respond violently—not that she would. But she understood the impulse.

Marjorie moved up in the line. It was shrinking much more quickly than she expected, but the anticipation of having to wait in two additional lines after this one dulled her contentment. She had already run through WAIT twice in her mind on the way to the DMV. Now that she had been there for over an hour, she did not feel like practicing her skills. And it still bothered her, the way Jessica had gotten off the phone so quickly this morning. Marjorie couldn't understand the difficulties in all her relationships; with Coryn, yes, but why was Jessica also pulling away? On the day she suggested therapy, Jessica had said something like, "You don't want to grow old alone, do you,

Marjorie?" Yes, her circle had shrunk, but it had never been large to begin with. As Mother Lydia said, whom did Marjorie have besides her sisters, who hated her? Where exactly was the Lord taking Marjorie, and was it somewhere so grand that it really couldn't accommodate any lasting love? Or was she, as Jessica thought, the problem? Was she really that volatile, Mother-Lydia-volatile?

And how could Marjorie tell her therapist not only of her affair, but also that it was not she, who, in holy wisdom, broke up with Charles, but he who rejected her, choosing Coryn over Marjorie once Coryn confronted him about the years-long relationship? Charles's rejection only solidified Marjorie's fear that there was something broken and ugly in her and irreparably so.

Maybe part of the reason Marjorie couldn't fully receive grace was that she didn't find the concept altogether fair. Why shouldn't some people be paid worse for their sins than others? Wasn't a child abuser much less forgivable than, say, a jaywalker or an adulteress? If sin was sin, why did Coryn, who also had an affair of her own and who stole from Mother Lydia and was promiscuous in every way, have so many of the things Marjorie wanted while Marjorie had so little to show for her thirty-seven years on earth and her thirty-three years of sanctification? Why did people like Coryn and Jessica—and even Latrice, who was born of the same biological mother and into the same circumstances—have it all, the marriages, the careers, the families, while Marjorie only got to be the cleanup woman with the burn marks? Yes, she was angry. Why shouldn't she be? And in the line, the weight of all this started to overwhelm her. She might at any moment faint or cry uncontrollably.

Marjorie stood at the front of the line now. The attendant, a brunette woman, smiled into Marjorie's face, the white collar of her shirt crisp and fragrant with fabric softener. Her nameplate said KELLY. She was downright perky, and this additional irritant Marjorie could not tolerate.

"Here to get fingerprinted, ma'am?" Kelly smiled. "I'll take that," she said, reaching for Marjorie's form. "The weather's supposed to be nicer tomorrow." She wore a purple glove on one hand. She grabbed Marjorie's thumb, manipulated it, and dipped it into the ink and onto the paper.

"I'd like to speak to a manager," Marjorie said as Kelly pressed her forefingers down.

Kelly smiled, confused, then noting Marjorie's facial expression, said, "Come again?"

"Your manager," Marjorie repeated. "I'd like to talk to a manager about the service in this place."

"I'm sorry you feel that way, ma'am. I can get a manager," Kelly said. "Can you tell me what the issue is so I can relay it accurately?"

It was as though she were reading from a script or an acronym on customer-conflict resolution, and that made Marjorie angrier. Kelly should speak to her like a real person, not a hypothetical scenario from a training manual. If anyone knew and understood these tactics, Marjorie did.

"I just said: the service," Marjorie raised her voice and looked behind her at the others in line for their corroboration, but no one would meet her eyes. She turned back to Kelly, lifted her hands in exasperation, and waited, watched her feelings, acknowledged her anger and sadness, imagined her options, noted the black ink all over her fingers, the many ways her heart and hands were still dirty, her sanctification stagnated, her plan to keep calm today thwarted, how her friends and even Charles were justified in their departures, the sad account she would give before the Lord.

And she proceeded to keep right on yelling as Kelly's smile faded and the customer lines parted to form a congregation around Marjorie's pulpit.

THIS TODD

This Todd was going to be different because he didn't insist that he was okay with his condition. He seethed, unapologetically, and he liked telling me how much he missed his legs, after a movie, before I climbed onto or off his lap, whenever I saw him slumped in his chair and the mood was ripe for melancholy. He didn't do any of that Pollyanna-before-the-fall stuff; he was Pollyanna right after the fall, and I liked that. He liked talking to me about it; he needed me to listen. My head filled the crook of his shoulder like a plinth for the Venus de Milo.

. . .

The first Todd's name was Brian, and I met him at the mechanic's. I sat in one of those polyvinyl chairs waiting for these men, who pretended they weren't talking down to me, to fix whatever was wrong with my car and to change my oil, because a good way to make them think you know something about cars is to get your oil changed. The waiting area smelled of rubber and stale coffee, and to avoid the lady across from me who complained—to me and the television—about the president's stance on women's healthcare,

I stared at the calves to my left. A purple rash interrupted their smooth brown and wrapped itself around the man's Achilles tendons—maybe lower, but I couldn't see below the socks or sneakers—and then ended, like a farmer's tan, right at the place where his shorts were hemmed.

He used a cherrywood cane with an ebony fritz, beautiful materials. I hate those offensive people who're all, "How did you become handicapped?" or, "What's wrong with you?" so I decided to make some small talk that might encourage him to voluntarily tell me about his condition. I still don't know what to call any of these guys—"differently abled," "disabled," "gimps," with an emphasis on reappropriating the term for good—so I just call all three of them Todds because that makes sense to me. Even now that their likenesses and eccentricities have formed a frieze around the upper walls of my mind, I still find them nearly interchangeable, except for this Todd.

The first Todd, Brian, laughed when I told him his cane looked really expensive and asked if I could touch it. "What kind of icebreaker is that?" he said. Then he told me his name and that I had "no game." That he would respond to a girl clearly out of his league with such confidence, to assume she was the one hitting on him, surprised me.

We talked until his car was ready. I liked the sinewy veins in his legs above the purple and the way his jaw clenched when he seemed to be thinking. His taupe eyes were rimmed with hazel. "I'll call you," he said, and I said, "Right," in my incredulous but still-flirtatious voice. When he stood and applied pressure to the cane, I saw that he walked off balance, his torso rocking from side to side like the eyes on one of those Felix the Cat clocks. I prayed his phone would die and somehow lose my number, but when he called, sounding so confident, so casual, I remembered why I had given it to him.

. . .

When I picture this Todd—not Brian, but this Todd, the third—I see his neckline, edged up so neatly you would think someone used a straight razor instead of clippers; he is always seated with his back to me, a slight cock to his neck, like he is looking upward, toward something better.

. . .

Dating a Todd wasn't that weird. Initially, it took a lot of adjusting on my part. I hesitated before introducing the first Todd to my friends, in case they did something to make him feel alienated or special. My friends aren't always as sensitive as I am. I considered arriving really early to everything so that Brian would already be seated and no one would see him hobble in, just to avoid the awkwardness, not because I was embarrassed. I resolved that there would be no dancing. Yes, his pants would cover the contusions, and he could probably make the sway look like swag if he stood in one spot. But at the time I worried about the stigma of the cane. Unless "Big Pimpin' " came on at the club—and why would it?— the cane would be a dead giveaway.

Everyone loved Brian, though, and I thought I did, too. We talked about regular grad school things, his interests in anthropology and autoethnography. He understood my sculptures and my latest montage, and I pretended to listen when he talked about normative whiteness and invisibility and cultural insensitivity. There was no paralysis to overcome. We parked easily when we carpooled to campus and enjoyed accelerated access to rides at

Disneyland before they stopped letting people do that—because believe it or not, some people will fake a handicap to get advantages. People actually hired their own Todds to move through the lines. I got used to his wheelchair, which he used on extended trips, and was soon comfortable operating it, leading him, pushing him with ease. I liked watching him struggle to pull on the compression socks he wore to bed. I liked the way the "flesh color" of the heavy fabric contrasted against the shades of brown of his skin, mottled as it was from the bruising and swelling, as if someone had stroked and wrenched and twisted the legs and squeezed the dark meat of them into pale casings. I tried to imagine rendering the image in sculpture, but could never settle on the right materials.

OF COURSE THERE were problems with Brian. I tried to make myself available for him as much as possible, not just sexually, but emotionally. But he could never balance his optimism about himself with his need for help. He was always like, "Kim, I really don't need any help." "Kim, my legs don't define me." "Please don't introduce me that way, Kimmy." "Kim, it's like some kind of fetish for you." "No, Kim, I don't want to play candy striper. No, you can't remove the bandages."

When he broke up with me, Brian said, "I don't want to hurt your feelings, but you're too clingy. I like a girl who has her own thing going on."

I could do so much better than him, so I told him to get to stepping. I felt justified by the slight wince in his brow.

I knew two weeks ago that this Todd was planning to leave

me. I'm not one of those women who would pleasepleasebaby-don'tgo. I am too valuable for all that. There's this saying I say: "Hit them where it hurts."

. . .

The second Todd I met on the bus, and he's a little crazy, so I'll call him Jamal to protect my identity. And for full disclosure, I didn't exactly need to ride the bus, because my car was fine by then, but I wanted to, occasionally, just to see who was on it. I sat in the front, near the handicap seats. I noticed his arms first, dark and ripped, contrasting against his green tank top. Then I noticed the walk. He had sort of limped onto the bus, and you could tell it wasn't an injury sort of limp, but more like a stiff gait, like he dragged his legs behind him, like Igor upright. His legs seemed especially thin, even in the jeans, child's limbs playing dress-up in a man's pants. He wore oversize headphones and insisted on standing the entire ride, even when I motioned that he could take the empty seat next to me. I thought that maybe he liked forcing himself to stand to build his leg strength, but I learned later that he just wanted to show off his arms by keeping them flexed as he gripped the bus handle. He nodded his acknowledgment of me in between bobbing his head to a beat, and I tried not to stare at the too-big jeans or overcompensating arms. I imagined under those jeans a stump, prosthetics, skeletal, underdeveloped legs with burns so bad the skin had turned to bark that would flake off with rubbing. But Jamal's legs were like nothing I'd ever seen before. Like Slim Jim jerky sticks on a wide torso, a GI Joe action figure ripped apart and scrunched onto Barbie's pins.

. . .

This Todd, not Brian, not Jamal, but the most recent Todd, the
one I envision looking upward, also had overdeveloped arms, and
when he was in a playful mood, he could lift me at least two
inches off his lap with one hand.

. . .

"This is becoming, like, a thing for you," Chelsea said the night
after she met Jamal.

"What is?"

"Don't play. These guys." She flicked her outdated side-
swooped bangs away from her eye.

"It's not a thing," I said.

"At least they've been hot so far."

"What else would they be?"

She rolled the eye I could see. "But it's kinda weird, girl. You
know it is, like it's becoming your thing."

Chelsea worked as a nurse and had improved her figure in the
past two years, but she continued to date a string of fake thugs,
all of them rehearsed just enough to seem ghetto but thoroughly
unfrightening, all of them spending their questionable income on
cell phones and sneakers instead of down payments for homes.
"Who's talking?" I said. "And it's not a thing."

"You're not fooling anybody. If you've got a thing, you've got
a thing. Just admit it. You always like to be the one in control."

"That's bull. Shut up," I said.

I BROKE UP with Jamal the day he looked like he was going to
put his hands on me. We had argued at his place over his un-

willingness to use his wheelchair all the time. "But don't you feel self-conscious, always limping so slowly behind me?" I asked as gently as I could.

I can't say for sure if he would have hit me, but I sensed his hand reaching for my neck. I could have taken a lesson from Wynonna Judd and pushed him and his wheelchair off the porch and said, "Come and git me, then, gimpy boy." Or I could have done a *Burning Bed* kind of thing and burned his bed, or gone all *Misery* on him and hacked away until he had no working limbs to ever try to lay on me again. But instead, I ran to my car, broke up with him over the phone later that night, told him his marionette legs disgusted me, and blocked his number.

. . .

This Todd was Chelsea's "special friend" when we were in undergrad, and I don't want to say she's a gold digger, but he bought her a lot of nice handbags and shoes and took her to the Ivy, and drove a Beamer even after it was too small to accommodate his wheelchair, yet she didn't call him her man. I'd known him before his tour in Afghanistan and never thought twice about him, although I regarded him as kind and not unattractive. He came back sullen and a little mouthy. He told Chelsea he wasn't into material things anymore, that disability checks were earned, that he needed someone who could understand that, whatever it meant.

He looked so bronzed and stately that evening we double-dated for dinner, before he broke up with Chelsea, before Jamal broke up with me. I'm not talking FDR in his chair, but London Paralympics, golden man, erect. My own personal Jimmy Brooks, my own Lieutenant Dan. He wore jeans with the legs hemmed to cover the nubs of his knees, his body bulky, even with the missing parts.

I was wrong to imagine clean cuts, the skin on the stumps like French-polished walnut. It looked more like the thread of a base-ball caked with clay and burnished dark, textured.

. . .

I'm trying to put this together the best way I can. The thing is, if this Todd could have just gotten used to things, learned to see the world in a slightly different way, seen a counselor to help him deal with his condition, we'd have been fine. If he'd actually applied for those grad programs in disability studies, if he'd had more to do than think about our relationship, we would have made it.

Todd got really mad at me, completely overreacted one day at Venice Beach, and it was the beginning of the end. A few weeks before, he said he didn't think we should move in together, yet. I noticed the wide space between "together" and "yet."

He hadn't been to Venice since before his second tour, and it was one of those days when the beach is so cold, all you want to do is sit close to someone and build a bonfire and make your own humidity.

When he was a kid, Todd's dad would take him to Venice a couple of times a month to watch the street performers and ride the Ferris wheel. Todd grew up near Huntington Beach, but his dad preferred Venice, "where all the color is." They'd get hot dogs with extra onions and mustard and eat them while they walked along the shore.

I'd wanted to surprise him, make him feel better after the problems we'd been having, but before we even reached the exit on the 10, he guessed where we were going.

"Babe, what are you doing?" He placed his palm over my knuckles as I shifted gears and merged right.

"We'll just have a nice day, walk around." I stifled the urge to correct myself. None of the Todds liked when I did that.

"I don't want to have to push against a big crowd today," he said, and I could tell he was in one of those moods, the kind where you couldn't reason with him much or he'd just shut down.

I already had to practically beg him to let me take him anywhere. "I'll clear all the people out of the way for you by making a beeping sound like a truck backing out," I said.

"And I'll be sure to run over your foot."

"Come on. We're here now. We can get some gelato and frozen lemonade, maybe a hot dog. I'll let you buy me a fake Chanel purse."

He smiled with one corner of his mouth. I snagged a sweet handicap space between the best side of the pier and the Ferris wheel.

THE WEEK BEFORE the beach, when I stayed over at his place, he'd asked, out of the blue, "Can you stop doing that?"

"Doing what?"

"Staring at them."

I had rested my head on his stomach, examining the cracks in the scar where one of his legs used to be, but I played dumb when he called me out. "What?"

He sat up and wriggled my head away from him. "Would you even date me if things were reversed?"

I sighed, dramatically, because I didn't want to get analytical. "You mean if I had no legs—" I tried to invert the image of us—me hunched in a wheelchair with ebony trim, like a defeated Blanche Hudson, only black and young and more beautiful, him hovering over me, studying the striations of the wounds.

He interrupted, "I mean if you had no legs, and I always re-minded you of it, or if you had, like, really bad skin, and I always stared at it, pretending I'm looking at something else."

"I don't do that," I said. "If anything, I remind you of how spe-cial you are, not special-special, you know, but, like, great-special."

"You don't get it," he said.

"Get what?"

"It's—it's like you always expect me to be grateful, like you're doing me a favor."

Later, I thought, wasn't that what he did when he bought Chel-sea and all the girls before me all those expensive things? At the time, I said, "Grateful for what?"

"That's exactly what I'm saying," he said, and rolled over with his back to me. A cold stump bumped against my calf under the covers.

HE BOBBED HIS head and threw a fiver at three break-dancing kids, and I knew we would have a good time. He fit awkwardly into most of the shops, even with ramps, but the foot traffic on the pier parted easily for us, anticipating the space of the wheelchair, making a clearing. People smiled directly at us. I wished Todd had worn his uniform, but he never wore it anymore.

The gasp of a little girl disrupted my bargaining with a street vendor who swore her carvings were made of real balsam. The little girl wore pink barrettes and took her finger out of her mouth to point at Todd's legs, or the lack of them. "Look," she said. Her mother nodded without acknowledging Todd. "Look," the girl repeated, now tugging her mother's sweater.

Todd said nothing. He could be passive in public.

I intervened. "Look," I mocked. "Look. What a funny-looking girl. You should really teach your kid how to behave," I said to the mother. "He's a real person."

The mother smacked her lips and got up in my face, but I didn't hear what she said because Todd grabbed my arm so hard that I almost fell into his lap.

"She's fine," he said to the mother. "Sorry about this."

"Why are you apologizing to her?" I started to get a little loud, but this was justifiable anger. The mother made unintelligible sounds as people stared.

"We're fine. Excuse me, everyone." Todd wheeled away. I had no choice but to follow.

We plowed on silently then, the crowd sluggish, blocking the path.

"Can we still get a hot dog?" I asked after a while, bending to look into his face.

Todd pinched his lips together so tightly it looked like his teeth were gone, too.

"Please, it's all I wanted for the day."

We ordered two hot dogs with mustard and onions from a man who played Turkish or Kurdish or maybe Indian music from an old stereo.

"Let's sit by the water." I beckoned my hand toward the shore, which rippled about one hundred yards away from the concrete path.

"You know I can't wheel over there."

A family of four looked both ways and crossed over the bike path. They paused at the line demarcating the sand to take off their shoes before sinking their feet in soft heavy steps.

"One day we'll get you one of those special all-terrain chairs," I said.

He made a noncommittal sound, not unlike a grunt, and said, "It's too overcast."

TODD DIDN'T LOOK at me once during the ride home. "Chelsea told me this wasn't going to work," he said quietly, as we approached the elevator to his apartment.

"You'll feel better tomorrow," I said.

. . .

For the next two weeks, I worked on something to make this Todd get it. Relying on my memory and intuition, I guesstimated the dimensions of his legs, the length and girth. I bought the wood— and with more money I hoped to buy a fancy set of sockets and connectors. I carved and sanded and massaged the wood and plied and buffed and blew off the dust and buffed again. I engraved the soles of the feet with my signature and distinctive paraph.

But the legs were so heavy, far too heavy for Todd to ever use them. I couldn't sand the insides down smooth enough to keep them from splintering and poking his skin. And it was too hard to line the sockets of the thigh with foam to cushion his bone prominences, so I focused most on the outside of the legs. Since Brian, I had criticized companies that didn't make tights or foundation to match dark skin and instead copped out by settling on light, dark, and medium, but I understood then. It isn't just white normativity, which is a concept Brian taught me. I tried so hard to match Todd's subtle skin tones, scumbled the legs with sepia and umber and chestnut. But even after a decade of studio work, I couldn't get it right. I can only hope that in a few years I can build a better model with a 3-D printer.

As I carried them up the stairs of Todd's apartment building—I never used the elevator except when I was with Todd—one leg dropped and thumped and clunked, scuffing itself along the stucco wall the whole way down, but I kept walking so that Todd could at least see part of what I had made. One leg is better than none.

"What are you doing here?" He looked frightened and rolled backward a few paces from his kitchenette set, I suppose because I didn't call before I used my key, but I knew he would be home.

"I told you things would get better," I said, presenting my labor, an emblem of my love for him, the symbol of my ability to overlook his shortcomings.

I left before the police arrived, making sure to grab the leg I had dropped. Todd screamed things I won't repeat; the neighbors came out of their apartments to watch.

. . .

A couple of times since then, I've tried to sleep with the legs tucked next to me under the covers—I put compression socks on them, I pose them just so.

The last time Chelsea spoke to me, she said, "But why? Doesn't that highlight how much of the whole person is missing?"

"No," I said. Chelsea could be dense sometimes. "He was the wrong Todd. I just have to find the right fit."

A CONVERSATION ABOUT BREAD

Junior was always trying out white folks stuff and bringing it to school for us to try. He wasn't built for Jackson, Mississippi. There were things black people just weren't supposed to do, like get caught on the wrong side of County Line Road after dark or use the word "persnickety," and Junior did both of those things, among others.

When he brought potato bread to school for lunch, we were all like, what's up with the yellow bread? For it was surely some white folks stuff and the dumbest thing we'd ever heard of until we tasted it. Once that yellow soft hit our mouths, though, it was like Apple Jacks; it didn't even have to taste like apple, or potato.

Croissants, too, not those pop-can crescent rolls our mamas and the lunch ladies tried to feed us. Junior had real croissants—the kind where you aren't supposed to pronounce the "r"—from a little bakery at the edge of the Fondren District. We ate the flaky edges of those croissants like they were Pop Rocks, just doing all their work in our mouths.

But most of us drew the line at brioche.

"See, this is why I don't tell you things." Brian angled the laptop away from his side of the table, and looking around the library, lowered his voice. A blond woman in a gray sweater—who looked like a librarian but wasn't one—stared from the adjacent table. "You're writing this like you're a white anthropologist." He mouthed the word "white" so that it made barely any sound, just an outline, like an expletive edited from a song. "We had croissants, the real kind, and we didn't eat those pop-can desserts, ever. We made things from scratch. And, Eldwin, did you just compare bread to Pop Rocks?"

Eldwin made his mouth a straight line and pulled the laptop away to reread.

"Why do you want to tell this story anyway?" Brian asked.

"Just tell me more about Junior and what you all ate. You know the assignment."

The brief ethnographical assignment required each student to collect an interesting story from another student in the class and decide which details to recount in order to form a profile of both person and region.

"I do know the assignment," Brian said, rolling his eyes. He looked young for his age. Only the deep-set horizontal wrinkle bisecting his forehead gave his age away. "If you want to write about race and food and whatever you think black Mississippians didn't have, I would say bagels. I feel like bagels were only in white neighborhoods."

"Bagels are everywhere," Eldwin said while his fingers worked the keys. "There's nothing explicitly or exceptionally white about them now, if there ever was—maybe Jewish at some point. But, I mean, everyone eats bagels now, and they aren't as sexy as croissants. Hold on a second." Eldwin didn't alter his volume when he said the words "white" or "Jewish." He typed for another minute or so. He was two shades lighter than Brian, but also believed himself two shades blacker, as far as those things can be measured. "How's this?"

Junior was always trying out white folks stuff and bringing it to school for us to try with him. He wasn't built for Jackson, Mississippi. There were things black people just weren't supposed to do, like get caught on the wrong side of County Line Road after dark or use the word "persnickety," and Junior did both of those things, among others.

When he brought potato bread to school for lunch, we were all like, what's up with the yellow bread? Dumbest thing we ever heard of until we tasted it. Once that yellow soft hit our mouths, it was like Apple Jacks; it didn't even have to taste like apple, or potato.

Bagels, too, shined up like soft pretzels. He actually asked the lunch lady, Ms. Martin, to toast them for him behind the counter, like we could do more than line up and eat the wet dog food they slopped onto our Styrofoam plates. But she did it for him, and we watched him take his little Tupperware container of Philadelphia cream cheese out of his bag and spread it over the hot bagels, and we pretended not to want a pinch so we wouldn't look like we were begging for somebody else's food.

But most of us drew the line at brioche.

Brian closed his eyes after he finished reading and pushed his wheelchair back a few inches from the table. "What exactly is 'yellow soft'? It sounds contrived, like you're trying too hard to sound country. No one would have said that, and on second reading I don't like the way you're representing the school."

"What's wrong with the school?" Eldwin said, scanning his work.

"It sounds like a prison-industrial complex."

Eldwin tugged at his unkempt goatee, twirling the coils into a severe point. He was the kind of guy who thought the gesture made him look smarter and that the goatee made him look older.

"It kind of *was* a prison-industrial complex," he started. "All those kinds of public schools are, and the private ones are part of the system in their own way." Eldwin was also the kind of guy who said "the system" often.

"I get that," Brian said, looking back at the white lady, who did not seem especially interested in the conversation, but who responded to Brian's attention by slumping farther into her book. "But I don't like the way it sounds when you write it," he said, smoothing his black polo shirt. He never wore blue or red, a phobia he'd picked up as a young child watching movies about Compton.

"How would you put it, then?" Eldwin said without looking up.

"I don't know. I'm not sure I would use the royal 'we.' I'd do more to try to distinguish the narrator from the other characters so it's not like they're some kind of monolith." Brian looked back at the white lady, and indeed she looked impressed by his use of the word "monolith."

They were both grad students in the Department of Anthropology at UC Riverside, occupying an atypical—almost magical—cohort that happened to include two black men. Their assignment required a combination of face-to-face interviewing and casual conversation, the field notes from which would form the sketches. It was Eldwin's turn to talk to Brian. They had agreed to write about Brian's time in Jackson—his current court case and disability were off-limits, Brian made clear—but Eldwin wasn't interested in either anyway; he wanted to pursue a story that Brian had told him months before, about a kid who brought potato bread to school. It was also Eldwin's idea—against the conventions of the assignment—to use first-person plural.

"I'm not writing about all black folks, or even all black people in Jackson," Eldwin said. "I'm representing a specific group, this 'we,' and I'm not trying to make that we an 'everyone.'"

"But in choosing the plural and the first-person plural you're basically allowing that 'we' to work as an 'everyone.'" Brian looked back at the woman and rotated his chair an inch away from the table, then back and away again.

Although both men felt like unicorns in their grad program, Brian had the most trouble with his horn, adjusting it nervously. He never apologized for his body; he was more self-conscious about his black maleness than his disability, though he felt at times that his cane, the wheelchair, and the contusions on his legs gave him a streak of rainbow hair to accompany the horn.

"You're on some respectability mess," Eldwin said without raising his voice, with the same tone he might use to say, "There's ketchup on your shirt." "It sounds like you're not as concerned with protecting black Southerners as you are with white people reading this and then making assumptions about black Southerners."

BRIAN WAS BORN in California, but he'd moved to Mississippi with his mother as a toddler, then back to the Inland Empire after his sophomore year of high school. He was tired of answering why, after living in California, he would ever consider moving back to Mississippi. People asked him more about that than his legs. He saw both states as home and liked the additional resources of SoCal, but he missed the smell of Yazoo City, his grandmother's acres of walnut trees and blackberry bushes. He found "native" Californians smug and condescending, and he found their suggestion that their drought-prone home was better than everywhere else in the world vapid. Brian had started at UCLA, a beautiful campus with more prestige, but he had to leave the university, the entire county, because of a stalking incident involving an artist named Kim and the ongoing litigation thereof. UCR was a step below his original PhD program but the department was paying for his degree, and the campus was easier to navigate in a wheelchair, which he used on longer days instead of his trademark ebony cane; the commute from San Bernardino to Riverside, though ugly, was manageable.

"It's not respectability anything," Brian started. "There's no real way for you to capture the regional differences without getting all stereotypical. Californians always think everybody else is less evolved, so no matter how conscious you think you are, you're still reproducing that false superiority. It's in the voice and"—he paused—"I don't know how you would say it—the occasion for the story. Like why it's being told in the first place. Like, why would you want to tell this story about a bunch of black Southern guys discovering bread anyway? What purpose does it serve unless it's to show yourself as somehow better than them?"

"Because it's a good story," Eldwin said, "about cultural differences, intraracial differences, class differences. It's more about how many different kinds of black people there are than it is about making everyone but Junior seem like a type." He seemed proud of this explanation.

The men worked without speaking for several minutes, Eldwin returning to his computer and Brian fiddling with his book but not really reading.

. . .

"You want it to seem that way." Brian put the book down.

"What way?" Eldwin asked, still tapping at his keyboard.

"The whole regional and intraracial thing you said, but it's like when my mom went to undergrad at USC. She had just moved here from Jackson, and she had this white roommate. She had dealt with white people before—her best friend in high school was one of the only white girls at the school—"

"So she was like an honorary black girl, then?"

"But my mom had never lived with any white people. And this roommate, Sandy, Mindy, something, was always trying to take pictures of my mom when she got out of the shower, when her hair was wet."

"Was the roommate a lesbian? Your mom was a lesbian?" Eldwin was excited now.

Brian cut his eyes. "So she could catch her in her 'natural state.' The girl was sending the pictures home to her family, like, look at this elephant I saw at the watering hole or this native with a disc in her lip."

"That's messed up," Eldwin said. "Was the roommate blond?"

"I don't know." Brian intensified his frown. "Probably not. But yeah, my mom threatened to fight her, and she brought a couple of her friends for backup, and the girl cried. Typical stuff. She never took another picture of my mom though, and I think she got transferred to another room second semester."

The white woman across from them looked amused.

Eldwin typed something.

"Wait, are you writing this down?"

"I'm taking some notes, that's all."

"The point of the story," Brian sighed, "is don't be that woman. You're acting just like her."

"I get it," Eldwin said, but he was still typing.

Brian sighed, dragging out the syllables of his irritation. "Let me ask you something," he said. "You were okay with not writing about my ex, Kim, or my court case."

"Right," Eldwin said. "You asked me not to; anyway, I wouldn't touch crazy Kim."

"Why is that?" Brian said, wheeling himself back toward the table a little.

"It's not my story, not open access. Didn't Kim have some kind of fetish? Didn't she treat you like fragile art?"

"Word," Brian said. "If I were in disability studies, I could write a whole dissertation on her and disability as fetish and the importance of self-narrating and all that."

"How is the stalking case going?" Eldwin said, finally looking up.

Brian shook his head and resettled his wheelchair at the table. "It's going. Anyway, you understand the issue with my mom's roommate and why my case isn't your story to tell, but you can't see how you're being a Kim with this bread thing?"

Eldwin paused at "being a Kim." His name was supposed to be Edward, the family lore held, but his illiterate grandfather botched the spelling on his birth certificate. He felt more like an Eldwin anyway. Brian didn't know that story, and Eldwin wasn't going to share it now.

"I'll be back," Brian said, leaving his stuff on the table and disappearing, after a moment, into the stacks.

If Eldwin cared about the white woman—and he might have at some level, but it wasn't a visible level—he would have seen that she was now very interested in the conversation. His theory, he had told Brian before, involved learning to ignore the white gaze until it no longer came to mind. Then, "and only then," he'd said, "black people can be free from all that double consciousness bull." If he cared about the white gaze or returned it with his own, Eldwin would have seen the woman take out a little notebook with a pink cat on the cover.

ELDWIN HAD ATTENDED a multiethnic charter school in Riverside and undergrad at Pomona College, where he supplemented his scholarship money with three part-time jobs. Grad school was paid for with a fellowship and teaching, and that gave him more time—or simply more opportunities—to practice being what Brian and others in his life described as smug.

His revised sketch read:

Me and Junior, see, hadn't been friends to begin with, until he brought that soft yellow bread to lunch one day. When he brought potato bread to school, I was like, "What is that? Who eats that?" But once it hit my mouth—a little yellow heaven.

He brought bagels, too, shined up like soft pretzels. He actually asked the lunch lady, Ms. Martin, to toast them for him behind the counter, like we could do more than eat

*the dog food they dumped onto our Styrofoam plates. But
she did it for him, and after I watched him take his little
Tupperware container of Philadelphia cream cheese out of
his bag and spread it over the hot bagels, I begged my mom
to buy me some, too.*

*Then there were other breads, brioche, challah—maybe
not challah—but raisin bread with the six or seven grains in
it. Junior and I became fast friends, eating lunch together,
playing basketball. But I drew the line when he wanted to
start a "gourmet club" at school. He was back on that white
folks stuff and maybe some gay stuff, too.*

Eldwin felt the sketch sounded worse than before. He wasn't
sure anymore why he wanted to tell this story in the first place or
if it was even possible to do ethnography without "being a Kim."
Didn't every story provide a narrow representation at best and fe-
tishize somebody at worst? He thought of his grandfather and his
name, how a misspelling had formed his identity. And why had
his mother let his grandfather dictate the birth certificate anyway,
knowing he couldn't read? Could no one in the hospital spell "Edward," or was that just a story the family told?

. . .

Brian returned from the stacks with two books and pushed one,
Frantz Fanon's *Black Skin, White Masks*, across the table to Eldwin.

"Cute," Eldwin said.

"You should really read it," Brian said.

"I will as soon as you read *Mumbo Jumbo*," Eldwin said, and
they both laughed a little, though neither man thought the situation humorous.

Eldwin clasped his hands together and stretched his fingertips over and behind his head.

"Did you finish the assignment?" Brian tugged at the laptop from across the table.

Eldwin resisted, pulling it back. "It's not ready."

"You've almost got a full page now."

"It's not ready," Eldwin repeated, and his face looked different, maybe sheepish. "Look, maybe you should tell this story yourself, and I'll write something else, some other school story; you pick," Eldwin said.

Brian shrugged. "Fine with me. You didn't even have to read the Fanon book to get right." He smiled.

The white woman, whose sweater was now draped over the back of her chair, looked flustered. She was taking notes but paused. She may have been an anthropologist, too.

WASH CLEAN THE BONES

Alma kept her eyes shut as she sang inside the church and later at the burial site. There was something about a closed casket that made her anxious, left too many gaps for her imagination to fill in. She tried to focus on her song. Thirteen. The boy was the same age as the number of bullet holes in his body, from head to torso.

The January wind whipped around her cheekbones but did not dry her sweat. She dabbed at her forehead with her silk scarf and caught her breath and sat in the white chair marked with her name. She did not feel her usual release at the pronunciation of "going up yonder," nor did the deep guttural sounds purge her grief. This was her fifth funeral in two months. Watching the pallbearers place white roses onto the silver casket, she felt guilty, suddenly, that she should be paid for participating in this intimacy. She didn't know this boy, though she knew three of the others she had sung for recently. Her fees kept her and baby Ralph outfitted in insulated winter coats, including the navy dress coat and matching beret she wore that day. Composed on the outside, inside she was falling apart. Her pelvis hurt; sweat dripped around the hairline of her best wig, and she couldn't warm herself inside the church or out on the sunlit lawn near the hole where they placed the boy and his box with finality.

"You sang," Bette, Alma's coworker from the hospital, said, meeting her with baby Ralph near the last row of chairs. "It was a nice service, lovely florals. And you sang."

The boy's mother, Mrs. Madison, approached and gripped Alma's hand silently, nodding approval before she departed with the rest of her family in the recessional line. She and her husband were in their early forties, and the boy was, or had been, their second-born son of four kids.

"Beautiful job. We'll see you at the house for the repast," a tall man, one of the uncles or cousins who helped with the burial, said from the moving line.

Alma smiled. She had worked the crowd; that was her gift, ironing out their sleepless stirring from the night before, if only temporarily. She performed "See You When I Get There" along with standard funeral fare. The boy's parents specifically requested that she avoid "I Believe I Can Fly." Funeral singing required the same skills she used to soothe friends in waiting rooms or console husbands at the bedsides of their wives. The crowd had "mmhmmd" and "amened" and sung along with "Since I Laid My Burdens Down" and waved their respective right hands in agreement with "sick and tired of being sick and tired." It had been a dignified funeral, without loud wailing or weeping, but something about the lack of the usual tensions—the absence of wailing or obvious signs of physical trauma—made Alma feel sick, the cold bloating her stomach like a fibroid, tying knots around her knots like so many adhesions.

The medications had caused her to gain twenty pounds in

two months, on top of the baby weight she hadn't lost from Ralph, and her original face floated in her new face. The gonadotropin and antidepressants her OB-GYN and colleague Dr. Brown prescribed weren't working to ease her pains, but she took them anyway to feel like she was doing something. She woke up drenched in cold sweats, kept fresh sheets and a clean gown in the nightstand next to her bed for 3:00 a.m. changes, could time the palpitations in her chest and the pains around her hip bones. They had induced early menopause at thirty-five to stop the growths, and these symptoms she had anticipated. What she didn't expect was the intensity of the night terrors; keeping her up after the sweats dried, creeping into her waking hours. And what was she to do about the baby, draped over Bette's shoulder, who was also sick and tired of being sick and tired and whose snot had caked and crusted around both of his nostrils so that all he could do was wheeze from his mouth, the baby who was appearing more frequently in her terrors?

"Let's get out of here," she told Bette.

· · ·

At the diner on Ashland, Alma and Bette settled into a booth and sat Ralph perpendicular to the table in a high chair. He whimpered, and Alma gave him the box of sugar and sugar alternatives to play with.

"You get his nose checked yet?" Bette said, stirring creamer into her coffee. She was a year older than Alma with no children of her own and often babysat Ralph when their shifts in the critical care ward didn't overlap.

"Same old thing," Alma said, staring into her tea.

Bette was saying something about how cute Ralph was and how his little dress shirt and burgundy tie made him look like an old man and how she could just eat him up.

You could have him, Alma thought. Then she said it out loud. "You could have him."

"And I would take him, too," Bette cooed at Ralph. "Yes I would, yes I would." She reached for one of the yellow sweetener packets, which Ralph had spread out on the high-chair tray. He grunted at her, snatching it back. "Be nice, Ralphie." Her voice sounded like the pink packets. "Be nice to Auntie Bette."

Alma made her own voice go high and light to affect the air of a hypothetical question. "But what would you do if I just left him, like at your doorstep?" She laughed a little.

Bette stopped smiling as she worked a packet out of Ralph's fingers, quickly emptied it into her coffee, and returned it to him. "I would take him, but I'd be concerned. What is it, Alma, the funeral, the funerals?"

"But how would you keep him safe?" Alma said.

"We live in a good neighborhood," Bette said, the other half of "we" referring to her husband, Justin. "Heck, you live in a good neighborhood."

"But how would you protect him?" Alma said.

"To the best of my ability," Bette started, but she finished with, "Maybe we should get back so you can get some rest. It's been a long week. I can take Ralph for the evening if you need a break."

Alma shook her head.

When they parted, Bette gave Ralph an extra hug and a "Be nice to Mama, sweetie," and said she would check in on Alma later.

. . .

In the terror from two nights before, Alma's brother Terry appeared with the boy from room 26, playing a guitar duet and singing a mish-mash of Terry's favorite old songs. Patches of dried blood checked the boy's faded green hospital gown like gunshot wounds, and though his dark skin looked pallid in the fluorescent lights of the room, he played the electric guitar vigorously, howling with demented fervor.

> *Oh, what's a man to do?*
> *What's a man to do*
> *If I can't have you?*
> *If I cant—*

They sang with none of Terry's typical levity when reciting the medley, their faces angry. The boy put his guitar down suddenly, and reaching into the breast pocket of his gown, pulled out a scalpel and approached Alma.

"I'm going to make an incision on your right side from about here to here," the boy said, pointing from one of his narrow hips to the other. "I'm going to pull you out a baby, name him something old-fashioned, like Ralph."

Alma looked to Terry for help, but he lay in the boy's bed with his eyes closed and his hands clasped together, as he had in his coffin. She tried to scream, but all that came out was a song. The nightmare ended abruptly with Alma drenched in her own blood, but when she touched her hips, there was only sweat.

. . .

Alma carried Ralph into her apartment, which overlooked a small man-made lake, and took off his coat. Ralph, eighteen months old and stocky, had stuffed four yellow and two pink sweetener packets into his pockets. He clutched a red coffee straw the entire ride home and even now in the house, and while she undressed him and wrestled with his nose and the aspirator, he sang in shrill but contented tones. "Go play with some of your toys, Ralphie," Alma said after she changed his diaper. She left the door to his bedroom cracked and settled into the eat-in kitchen.

Bette would think she was crazy; she should have told her about the lack of sleep, at least from the medication. The night terrors she would keep to herself. Terry frequently visited her in them, but increasingly lately so did her patients from the critical care unit, and even trauma patients she'd only heard about in the hallways but didn't actually work with were making appearances. They—Alma, her mother, her sister, Lisette, and Terry's girlfriend, Katrina—had buried Terry seven years ago at age twenty-nine after a shoot-out with the police. That was the term the papers had used, "shoot-out," but Terry had been unarmed. The legal cases were closed, his casket open, his nighttime visitations to Alma frequent but no longer alarming. He didn't seem to be trying to tell her anything she didn't already know about the circumstances of his death. She kept a piece of his femur wrapped in acid-free parchment in the downstairs closet. She had washed it clean herself, a personal request she had made of the coroner. Her mother and sister and Katrina had kept his other remains, clothes, books, guitars.

But why was he visiting with the children, the ones from the hospital? Three weeks earlier, it had been the boy who ran in front of the police car, two months ago a girl whose brother was playing with their mother's gun.

Ralph cried from behind the cracked door, wanting her to pick him up. And though he could walk—he was just stubborn—Alma picked him up and carried him into the family room, presenting him with two shortbread cookies and a paper plate full of cheese crackers.

Alma used to imagine her life something like sensual, frets and strings and wires that in the right combinations produced beautiful chords, slow, whining blues. Now it was also shrieks in the middle of the night and whimpering at a moment's notice. It was all bodies—the ones that came into her unit with bullet holes, kids as young as eleven and twelve, hoodies soaked—and the ones dressed for the funerals, their holes plugged and covered with their finest dress clothes, often purchased at the last minute by mothers struggling to keep spaghetti noodles with butter on the table.

When Alma first started at the hospital, some of the nurses taught her to pray for the children according to severity. A level one meant pray that the child would be well; level two meant pray for decreased pain. Alma was slow to understand level three—praying that the children would die, that mercy and grace would shorten their suffering—but she had come around to it a few months into her job, when the boy with the shattered face was wheeled in. His mother's eyes convinced Alma that sometimes you suffered more the longer you lived.

THERE WERE SO many bodies in Alma's everyday life, even Ralph's undersize one, alternately leaky then stopped up with bronchitis, bronchial infections, chronic sinus congestion that colored his nostrils green and yellow and made him throw up in the middle of the night to keep from suffocating. Alma would bathe him and try to go back to sleep, grateful that he hadn't choked.

THE PHONE RANG, and Alma debated ignoring Bette's call before she answered it.

"I'm okay," she insisted when Bette offered to come over. "I'm going to get us ready for bed early and enjoy my day off before it's over."

His birth certificate read Ralph Boaz Parr, but Alma called him her Samuel, because while her womb was still contorted around her bowel, she promised the Lord that if He blessed her with a child, she would offer the baby back up to Him. After two laparoscopic surgeries—one to remove a six-centimeter fibroid with teeth and hair—a D&C, and a round of fertility treatments, she conceived Ralph with the help of her friend Danny, who'd agreed to serve as a sperm donor but not a parent, as a father but not a dad. That was fine with Alma, then. Now the adhesions were back—she could feel them pull in her left side—and Alma took the drugs to delay another surgery. She wondered what might have happened if she had chosen to have a baby the traditional way, if Danny had been the dad, even the husband, and not just the father. She might have more support, or maybe Danny, finding the caretaking of Alma and Ralph unbearable, might have left her as alone as she was now.

Ralph had worn a white suit and bonnet to his christening, which Danny did attend, three months earlier, around the time the night terrors intensified. At the christening they hadn't fully immersed Ralph but sprinkled him with water and anointed his head with blessed oil, in the Pentecostal tradition. Alma kept a portion of the blessed olive oil in a narrow glass bottle etched with swirls under her bathroom sink.

Alma didn't go as far as her mother in her use of blessed oil. Her mother applied it to the posts of the house, walked around muttering incantations, and suggested that the baby could use a dab on his forehead if he started to act fussy. Still, for her performances, Alma anointed her own head with oil and said a quick prayer that she would, in humility, comfort these families and friends, that they would remember the encouragement of the lyrics, and be settled by the melodies. Without the oil—though she couldn't be sure of any of this—her performances seemed less palliating, and left grit in what should been salve. It's not that her songs sounded any less beautiful, but after she sang without the anointing, the families smiled at her and clasped her hands as though she were the one who needed consoling. Yes, she must have forgotten to use the oil before she sang her set at the Madison boy's funeral. That must be why, despite their compliments, she felt so unsettled.

"Let's get you in the bath," Alma said, turning on some music and carrying Ralph to the second bathroom.

. . .

That night, she applied castor oil to her abdomen, starting with her right side, massaging the liver, and working her way down her belly to each hip and then back to her flanks. As with the blessed oil, her body reminded her when she forgot to complete the ritual. The toxins seemed to accumulate faster, her digestion became sluggish, and the pain—which never fully left but liked to remind her it could become worse—wrenched around in her abdominal and pelvic cavities. The castor oil packs were supposed to shrink all the growths, the Internet said, and despite her research training and her misgivings, Alma coated herself with the cold, viscous oil each night and waited for signs of improvement. She laid a heating pad over herself and wrapped her torso in old cloths. The oil stained her sheets anyway, leaving a thick smell behind. That was her life, the residues you could wash out and the ones you couldn't.

She didn't sleep. She could never sleep after performances, no matter how well they went and especially now. She anticipated Terry and thought the Madison boy, under the lid of the casket, would accompany him. But it was Ralph who appeared with Terry in the terror this time, not singing but crying with a gravely voice, "How will you keep me safe?" His face and clothes were soaked, as though someone had submerged him in water.

Alma got up and checked on Ralph, who lay wheezing softly in his crib. When she returned to her room, she knelt at her bedside and said an extra round of prayers. She turned her television on mute and played music from her phone with the volume low. She sat upright in her bed and worried over her shift four hours away, her life, her pelvis.

WHEN ALMA STARTED as a wedding singer, single and childless, business was slow, but it was her passion, not just a side hustle; she didn't need the money. Some of her clients—who learned about her through word of mouth at the hospital and the sample CD she passed out during consultations—found her riffs and runs too much for the occasion, preferring something more Episcopalian than Church of God in Christ on their special day. As a funeral singer, she had more gigs than she wanted and paid for the fertility treatments on her own with the profits, though it seemed wrong to call them that.

Her sister and mother couldn't understand why Alma would go through the rigorous treatments to prep her womb only to be a single parent. But they never brought up the untraditional means by which Ralph was conceived once they saw "that precious baby boy, looking just like his uncle Terry."

Even detached as he was from her uterus, and even with her solid network of supportive family and friends, Ralph felt sometimes to Alma like another adhesion, a growth on her future happiness.

· · ·

Alma gave up on sleep and sat in the kitchen after she sensed Terry and Ralph coming to her once more. It was still dark out, and the lake rippled under a distant streetlamp. She checked on Ralph in his crib again. His diaper and the bottom half of his onesie were soggy, and something white and oozy curdled around his chest. Alma thought she might cry as she made her way to the second bathroom and drew a bath.

She should call Bette or maybe the hospital, or even her mother.

She did not pause to pull the baby tub that sat inside the larger one out of the cabinet. She ran water, testing the temperature with her elbow. She took Ralph from his crib, and he fussed and whimpered for a moment, then looked into her eyes as if to say, "Why did you wake me?"

She attempted to compose a text message in her mind, some sort of explanation or apology, but she couldn't settle on the right words. Ralph clapped his hands together before and after she pulled his shirt over his head. She undressed him and then dressed him in a white linen suit she had bought for an upcoming vacation trip. She blessed his forehead with olive oil.

A song came to her, something Terry used to play on his acoustic guitar when she was six or seven. She would get ready for work when she finished with Ralph—she could work on less sleep than this—and tend to the boy in room 47, maybe pray a level three for him and a level two for herself.

When she covered Ralph's head with the warm water, she reasoned that at least it wasn't freezing. At least it was shallower than the plunge from the side of a slave ship. At least it was more comfortable than forcing him to float down the Nile in a woven basket. She dunked him once and counted to five. Had there been time for Terry to cry out as the bullets shattered his right leg, his chest? Would she preserve any part of Ralph? Their faces were blurring together. She wept in terror and allayed her guilt by singing soft phrases, "his bones will be unbroken," "there'll be no more crying there." She could do this—eleven, twelve, thirteen. By fourteen, doubt had begun to creep in. Shouldn't Ralph have a choice, now that he was already here? Who was she to snuff out his life for fear that someone else would? Would Terry want this for his nephew?

She yanked Ralph from the water, his eyes wide, her count long lost. She feared the damage was already irreparable and listened to his chest. Alma was frantic, but the muscle memory took over, and she began pumping for CPR. What if her baby did not wake up, and even then, would he be vegetative for the rest of his life?

She had only pumped once when Ralph gurgled, spat water, and cried. He was used to barely breathing.

Alma exhaled for the first time in months.

She didn't know how they would get through the night, let alone years; one or both of them might end up with their heads underwater some other day. For now, she would monitor Ralph and herself, perhaps call Bette. She gently pinched Ralph's chubby leg. She felt something like sunlight on her neck and torso, saw a hot flash of heaven or hope in that baby's wet face, and redressed him and herself for bed.

AUTHOR'S NOTE

I would be remiss if I did not give credit for the title of this collection—and its titular story—to the writers who inspired it. The original "'The Heads of the Colored People,' Done with a Whitewash Brush" was written by James McCune Smith, under the pen name Communipaw. Smith created a long-running series of sketches similar to those mentioned in this collection's opening story and similar to the works of his contemporaries William J. Wilson (who wrote his own series of sketches called *The Afric-American Picture Gallery* mentioned in "Heads") and Jane Rustic (a.k.a. Frances Ellen Watkins Harper), a prolific black writer, abolitionist, and feminist. These writers published widely, often serializing their work in *Frederick Douglass's Paper*, *The Anglo-African Magazine*, and *The Christian Recorder*. Some of these works have since been anthologized in volumes like *A Brighter Coming Day*, edited by Frances Smith Foster. The sketches, first introduced to me in the work of the scholar Derrick R. Spires, narrate black life from the mundane to the obscure and span the didactic to the macabre.

This collection departs in most ways from the original content of the nineteenth-century black writers' sketches. The stories presented here do not follow the brevity of the sketch form. And while Smith, Wilson, and Watkins Harper were trying to theorize what it would mean for black people to have the full rights of citizenship, the black people in this collection have, on paper, full rights under the law. But like the original sketches, these stories maintain an interest in black US citizenship, the black middle class, and the future of black American life during pivotal sociopolitical moments. The stories herein also play with the theme of "Heads" broadly, considering literal heads as well as leadership and psychology. And as should be clear, this collection is just as preoccupied with black bodies and the betrayals of those bodies—both external and internal—as it is with heads.

SELECTED BIBLIOGRAPHY

Brown, Charles Brockden. "An Address to the Ladies, by their Best Friend Sincerity." *The American Magazine. The Charles Brockden Brown Electronic Archive and Scholarly Edition.* January 20, 2017. http://www.brockdenbrown.cah.ucf.edu /xtf3/view?docId=1788-07594.xml;query=;brand=default.

———. *Arthur Mervyn; or, Memoirs of the Year 1793: With Related Texts.* Edited by Philip Barnard and Stephen Shapiro. Indianapolis: Hackett Classics, 2008.

———. *Wieland and Memoirs of Carwin the Biloquist.* New York: Penguin Classics, 1991.

Cullen, Countee. "Incident." *My Soul's High Song, Collected Writings of Countee Cullen, Voice of the Harlem Renaissance.* Edited by Gerald Early. New York: Anchor, 1991.

Douglass, Frederick. *Selected Speeches and Writings.* Edited by Philip S. Foner and Yuval Taylor. Chicago: Chicago Review Press, 2001.

Fanon, Frantz. *Black Skins, White Masks.* Translated by Richard Philcox. New York: Grove, 2008.

Harper, Frances Ellen Watkins. *A Brighter Coming Day*. Edited by Frances Smith Foster. New York: The Feminist Press at CUNY, 1993.

Hatori, Bisco. *Ouran High School Host Club*. Volume 1. San Francisco: VIZ Media, 2005.

Kelly, Donika. "Arkansas Landscape." *Bestiary*. Minneapolis: Graywolf, 2016.

Lisis, Brian. "Virginia Man Brings Five Wheelbarrows Full of Pennies to DMV to Pay Taxes." *Daily News* (New York, NY). January 13, 2017.

Ohba, Tsugumi. *Death Note*. Volume 1. San Francisco: VIZ Media LLC, 2005.

Romero, Dennis. "Mystery of Mean DMV Worker Solved by USC Researchers." *LA Weekly* (Los Angeles, CA). September 23, 2011.

Smith, James McCune. *The Works of James McCune Smith: Black Intellectual and Abolitionist*. Edited by John Stauffer. Oxford: Oxford University Press, 2007.

Solomon, Asali. *Disgruntled*. New York, Picador, 2016.

Spires, Derrick R. *Black Theories of Citizenship in the Early United States, 1787–1861*. Philadelphia: University of Pennsylvania Press (forthcoming).

Tannenbaum, Rob. Playboy Interview: John Mayer. *Playboy*. February 2010.

Thurston, Baratunde. *How to Be Black*. New York: Harper Paperbacks, 2012.

Watsuki, Nobuhiro. *Rurouni Kenshin*. Volume 1. San Francisco: VIZ Media, 2008.

Wilson, William (Ethiop). *Afric-American Picture Gallery*. 1859.

http://jtoaa.common-place.org/introduction-afric-american-picture-gallery.

———. "Number 26." *Afric-American Picture Gallery. The Anglo-American Magazine: 1.* Edited by William Loren Katz. New York: Arno P. and the New York Times, 1968.

LIST OF PUBLICATION ACKNOWLEDGMENTS

"Belles Lettres," *Los Angeles Review of Books Quarterly* 13 (2017): 75–88.

"The Body's Defenses against Itself," *Compose*, November 1, 2015, http://composejournal.com/articles/the-bodys-defenses-against-itself.

"Fatima, the Biloquist: A Transformation Story," *Lunch Ticket*, June 17, 2016, http://lunchticket.org/fatima-the-biloquist.

"Heads of the Colored People: Four Fancy Sketches, Two Chalk Outlines, and No Apology," *Story Quarterly* 49 (2016): 117–27.

"The Necessary Changes Have Been Made," *The White Review*, (forthcoming).

"This Todd," *Blinders Journal*, January 1, 2015, www.blindersjournal.org/issue%20two/NafissaThompson-Spires.html.

"Whisper to a Scream," *East Bay Review*, November 1, 2015, http://theeastbayreview.com/whisper-to-a-scream-by-nafissa-thompson-spires.

ACKNOWLEDGMENTS

First, I want to thank God for this opportunity and divine timing and for the many people who helped make this collection possible: Derrick, my husband, I'm so proud of you and grateful for your ongoing love, support, and your brilliant work; my parents, Rufus and Dr. Gail Thompson, who kept books in my hands and love in our home and served as my first mentors, publicists, and editors; my siblings, NaChé and Stephen Thompson, and my nephews Iveren and Isaiah for keeping me laughing; my aunt and uncle Tracy and Thomas Harkless, my mother-in-law, Daisy Spires, and my aunt Merlene Walker for being cheerleaders and sending me useful things like avocados and flannel sheets; and my godmother Margaret Goss, who encouraged me to be a writer.

Friends, you are invaluable, especially Selena Brown.

Donika Kelly, Destiny Birdsong, Nikki Spigner, and Deborah Lilton, thank you for providing a safe space for our writing and yoga—and Petal Samuel and Kaneesha Parsard for enriching and shaping that space as it evolved.

Leah Rae-Mittelmeier Soule, Natalie Inman, Valencia Moses, Elizabeth Barnett, Diana Bellonby, Matt Duques, Jasper Spires,

Adrienne Coney, Debbie Harris, Shirleen Robinson, and Emily August, thank you for supporting me and my work.

To my many teachers, thanks for all you have sown into me: longtime mentors Paul D. Young, Carolyn Dever, and Dana Nelson, who nurtured me and Derrick through graduate school and beyond, listened to me talk ad nauseam about *Degrassi* and other Canadian things, and in some cases even gave us homemade pasta sauce; Ravi Howard and Jacinda Townsend, who workshopped a few of these stories and taught me to empathize more with my characters; Lorraine Lopez, Tony Earley, and Alice Randall, who provided excellent professional advice during my earliest days of creative writing; U of Illinois faculty mentors and colleagues Alex Shakar, Audrey Petty, LeAnne Howe, Steve Davenport, Janice Harrington, Robert Dale Parker, Candice Jenkins, and Ronald Bailey for believing in my work; the U of I departments of African-American Studies and Creative Writing more generally; and Mrs. Colleen Farley and Ms. Sandy Alps, my middle school and high school English teachers, respectively, who contributed to my love of writing.

Many thanks to the colleagues and friends who have workshopped these stories and other writing, particularly Avery Irons, Roya Khatiblou, Greg Rodgers, Kristin Walters, Nolan Grieve, and Katherine Scott Nelson; the Callaloo Creative Writing Workshop and Callaloo friends in general, especially Marame Gueye, Kiietti Walker-Parker, Toni Ann Johnson, Baleja Saidi, Anya Lewis Meeks, and Courtney Moffett-Bateau; all the Binders who have taught me things every day online and at BinderCon; and Allison Wallis.

Thanks to the magazine editors and writers who published individual stories, judged them in contests, or invited me to read, including Stefanie Sobelle, Arielle Silver, Joanne Yi, Medaya Ocher, Lisa Beth Fulgham, Suzannah Windsor, Reem Al-Omari, Caleb

Daniel Curtiss, Paul Lisicky, Stephanie Manuzak, Michael Sakoda, Jeff Chon, Jennine Capó Crucet, Peter Orner, and Mat Johnson.

Special thanks to Keith Wilson for letting me paraphrase his Facebook post about how black women die off camera and to Peter Hudson for saying "black crazy" in my presence but not about me.

With so much gratitude, thank you to my wonderful agent, Anna Stein, for believing in this project and editing it before it went out into the world and answering my many anxious emails, and on top of that giving me free books; to Madison Newbound, who has been very helpful and kind; to Mary Marge Locker, who worked on the book in its early days; to all the people at ICM who have made this happen; to Jensen Beach for putting me in touch with Anna and convincing me that short stories are still worth writing; and to my awesome co-agent Sophie Lambert, who sold the book in the UK; and all the folks at Conville and Walsh.

And finally, to my editors, Dawn Davis, Clara Farmer, and Charlotte Humphery, and to Lindsay Newton—a million thanks for your hard work reading and sculpting draft after draft, line after line. And thanks to all the people working behind the scenes in sales, publicity, copyediting, and art design at Atria/37 Ink and Chatto and Windus. There's no way this book would be what it is now without you, and I am forever grateful.

ABOUT THE AUTHOR

Nafissa Thompson-Spires earned a PhD in English from Vanderbilt University and a Master of Fine Arts in Creative Writing from the University of Illinois.

Her work has appeared or is forthcoming in *The White Review*, *Los Angeles Review of Books Quarterly*, *StoryQuarterly*, *Lunch Ticket*, and *The Feminist Wire*, among other publications. She is a 2016 participant of the Callaloo Creative Writing Workshop and 2017 Tin House workshop, and a 2017 Sewanee Writers' Conference Stanley Elkin Scholar. Born in San Diego, California, she now lives in Illinois with her husband.